Praise for *The New Me*

'*The New Me* renders contemporary American life in such vivid, stinging color, that certain sentences are liable to give the reader a paper cut. But you'll want to keep on reading anyway. Halle Butler is terrific, and I loved this book'
Kelly Link

'*The New Me* is a bouncy, profane, highly addictive novel about work, female friendship, and other alienations. Halle Butler's insane talent shimmers on every page of this dead-pan misanthrope's ode. A must-read!'
Claire Vaye Watkins

'Halle Butler has a way of looking at our 21st-century neo-liberalist condition that simultaneously exposes its brutality and renders that same brutality absurd, hilarious, fizzy with humor. She's an incisive, curmudgeonly bard of the uniquely precarious times we live in, and it is crucial that you read her immediately'
Alexandra Kleeman

'A bleak and brutal book that exposes a nearly unbearable futility to life in the workforce, not to mention life outside of it. Butler's vision is funny and raw and dark—a cautionary tale, hilarious and intimate, against growing up and making do'
Ben Marcus

'Halle Butler is a first-rate satirist of the horror show being sold to us as Modern Femininity. She is Thomas Bernhard in a bad mood, wearing ill-fitting tights, scrutinizing old take-out leftovers. *The New Me* shows us the futility of betterment in an increasingly paranoid era of self-improvement, one in which the female body is grated into little bloody empow-ered bits of itself. A dark comedy of female rage. Fucking hilarious'
Catherine Lacey

the new me

Halle Butler is the author of *Jillian*. She is a National Book Foundation '5 Under 35' honouree and a Granta Best Young American Novelist.

the new me

halle butler

WEIDENFELD & NICOLSON

First published in Great Britain in 2019
by Weidenfeld & Nicolson
an imprint of The Orion Publishing Group Ltd
Carmelite House, 50 Victoria Embankment
London EC4Y 0DZ

An Hachette UK Company

1 3 5 7 9 10 8 6 4 2

A CIP catalogue record for this book is
available from the British Library.

ISBN (Mass Market Paperback) 978 1 4746 1229 6
ISBN (eBook) 978 1 4746 1230 2

Printed and bound in Great Britain by
Clays Ltd, Elcograf S.p.A.

Text designed by Sabrina Bowers

FSC
MIX
Paper from
responsible sources
FSC® C104740

www.orionbooks.co.uk
www.weidenfeldandnicolson.co.uk

For Jerzy

I t's winter in Chicago.

In the windowless back offices of a designer furniture showroom, women stand in a circle, stuffed into ill-fitting black jeans, gray jeans, olive jeans, the ass cloth sagging one inch, two, below where the cheeks meet. They don't notice this on themselves, but they notice it on each other. They wear cheap suede ankle boots and incomprehensible furry vests that flap against them as they talk, pushing their voices out an octave too high, lotioned, soft, gummy hands gesturing wildly. One of them wears a topknot, another checks her pedometer.

Edwin McCain's "I'll Be" plays in the background. They are allowed to choose their own music.

They shift between subjects with a rapid ease, words spilling out of their mouths. One of them is explaining something from her real, nonwork life, something about returning something she bought online—the frustration and indignity of the experience.

The one in the topknot and a tunic looks down and laughs. "Oh my god you guys look at me I'm such a hipster." Another smiles, barely containing her disgust, and says "No, you look cute" with her words and "Oh my god shut the fuck up" with her eyes.

One of them leans over her immersion-blended meal, laughs with strain, and says, referring to a chandelier on the showroom floor, "Where I come from you can get a *house* for twenty thousand." A glob of green puree hangs from the fuzz on her mohair sweater, right by the boob. No one responds.

They start talking about a woman who works down the hall. She used to work here, and they all hate her. Apparently she really likes chrome and has no friends. One of them slides an open catalog across the table and says, "Isn't that so trashy?" It's a chrome coffee table, indistinguishable, to me, from the rest of the wares.

The whole scene is a bitter cliché, the expectations and ego barely hidden behind the flimsy presentation of friendliness.

My pits are slick, and my face smells like a bagel.

I wonder if I should chime in, tell them that I also think the table sucks, but the words catch in my throat. Impossible to join in, even if I wanted to, which I don't, not really.

I'm the new temp, ten days into my assignment here. I've been getting better temp assignments lately, and my rep writes to tell me things like "I'm so excited for you, this one has possibility for temp to perm," but so far perm hasn't come. I wonder how I would have to behave, how many changes I would have to make, to tip myself over the edge into this endless abyss of perm.

I walk home in the dark, in the snow. My tights sagging. A hole in the side of my shoe.

I open my dark apartment and turn on all the lights, like there might be someone who needs to use a room I'm not in. Like I'm expecting company. Like I still share my life.

I light a cigarette and open my laptop. I turn on an episode of *Forensic Files*, my favorite of the serialized murder documentaries, to comfort myself.

There's someone in the house!

I wish.

chapter 2

I t's a new day. I'm on the train, 8:45, still dark outside, hot, shitty outfit, hole in my underwear from scratching too much, an aimless bile rising at the back of my throat already, as usual, for no reason, like it always does, like I'm in an experiment, my face inches from a short woman's stupid hat, the poofball of the hat a clown's nose for me.

She's completely hogging the train pole, oblivious.

Her hat almost touches my face.

It's a Chicago Bears Breast Cancer Awareness stocking cap. Hideous on every level. The rest of her outfit another fuck-you disappointment, thick purplish tights, a knee-length down parka, boots with fur detailing that looks like a dead dog's stuffed down in there, the whole thing a real carefree snugglefest, a real assault, a real declaration of who this woman is, draped in death and violence and completely unaware of it. The perfect mix of compliance and violence.

I sigh, lean into her, give her the signals that she should look up, say oops, move to the side, but she stays there, lump-like, the brass placard of her mini backpack catching on my cheap secondhand coat. I imagine the mindless ease of her life. I imagine her thinking about that show she likes on ABC where adults pretend to be fairy-tale characters trying to make each other horny, and I imagine her referring to it as a guilty pleasure, like that's somehow radical or somehow makes her interesting. Will Rumpelstiltskin be able to trick Peter Pan into betraying his relationship with Snow White by reminding him of his long-ago love with the Little Mermaid? *I don't know, baby, will he??* I want to use my hands to redirect her face to a fucking mirror.

I make a decision, rare these days, and my arm goes out, right angle from my body, and I grab the pole so hard my knuckles turn white.

We ride like this for a second, my arm pressed firmly into the side of her head.

Inside of her idiotic hat, I can feel how small her skull is. I've been told that my skull is exceptionally large. I don't usually touch strangers' heads, and the feeling is intimate, thrilling. Her small, thin skull taps against my forearm. She's still not accommodating me. I press harder. I try to loom. She bends her head awkwardly out of my arm's way, making herself look even more innocent, even more compliant, like a good little girl, confronting me by not confronting me.

A man across the train looks at me like I'm the villain, and then he looks down. Now he's my enemy, too, how does he like that? I think the phrase "a symphony of bullshit" and

I get off the train. On the escalator, nobody stands on the right and walks on the left, and everything is wrong.

I enter the showroom, they're playing Coldplay, and I say "Morning!"

Karen, the senior receptionist, and technically my supervisor, smiles at me like I can't tell that she's faking, and says "Hi, Maddie" and I say "Hi!" but that's not my name. It's Millie, not Maddie. I want to go up to her and prostrate myself on her desk, my ribs activating her shitty gold stapler, the one I know she loves so much, over and over, by thrashing, spending staples all over her desk, while I explain to her the difference between Mildred and Madison. I want to press my nose into her keyboard and tell her that my parents both went to grad school, I was raised correctly and in a good home, and it's an insult to my mother, the professor, to imply that she named me Madison after the mermaid from fucking *Splash*, when I was named after my great-great-grandmother, a *suffragette*, you fucking thankless cunt, and in this fantasy, I become insensible and start crying, deep from the gut, which isn't much of a fantasy, as far as fun and variety are concerned.

I smile at Karen again, leave the front desk, and walk through the showroom, past the re-created, tasteless living spaces, to my station in the back offices.

There are donuts in the break room, and I eat one. No one is talking to me or looking at me, as usual. I say almost nothing, almost all the time. Obviously, I recognize, in a grander sense, that I have a tendency to alienate myself and blow things out of proportion, and that these women are basically guiltless from a certain perspective. I fully recognize the concept of perspective. The donut is down in my throat, a disgusting bolus, after two bites.

I recognize so much that it bores me. I recognize that the Formica is covering a slab of cheap wood pulp, and that, among the snacks in the refrigerator, some of them contain wood pulp. I know that the woman checking her phone in the corner, pretending I'm not here, is wrapped up in some distraction so utterly meaningless that it should, if she reflected on it, shake her to her core.

She takes a small piece of bread out of her pocket and places it in her mouth with two fingers, surgically precise.

I saw a woman at the Pret A Manger by the museum tear off tiny pieces of bread and place them at the back of her mouth once, almost putting her entire hand inside her mouth. It looked like it was supposed to seem elegant, and I wondered where she learned it. This reminds me of that.

None of this thinking does me any good, obviously.

As I walk back to my desk, a woman barges past me into the break room. We almost touch crotches, and I say, "Oop, sorry!"

My dirty coffee cup from yesterday is next to the dead bamboo plant from my predecessor. If I thought I'd be here more than a few weeks, I'd throw the plant away. Maybe go buck wild and get a desk calendar.

A woman, heralded by the clattering nuts in her snack-sized Tupperware, walks up to my cubicle and tells me she likes my shirt—a pure bluff, it's a pit-stained silk J.Crew af-fair, too tight and five years old—and asks me if I need any help, but all I do is answer phones and assemble packets of junk mail, so I say, "No, not really, I'm all good," and smile and wait for her to leave. Her name is, I think, Lindsey. Pos-sibly Rachel.

Everyone takes a long time explaining simple things to me, like they're afraid of me, like maybe I've never seen a landline before, like there's something I'm going to do to fuck this up, even though, of course, I've had jobs before. Many of them.

On my first day, Karen showed me how to turn on a computer, then looked at me with kindness and said that it could be kind of tricky, so maybe I should write it down. I nodded, and while I was writing it down, she said, "You're the front lines here, and our phones are an important part of our business, so if you could try to time your bathroom breaks with your lunch break, that would be great. Unless it's an emergency, of course."

Yes, of course.

I'm drinking burnt coffee and googling foods that reduce stress when the phone rings, a real asshole on the line.

"Lisa Hopper, how may I direct your call?" I say.

"I'm outside!" he says, shouting in a distracted way.

"I'm sorry?" I say.

"I'm standing outside," he repeats, slowly. My confusion about what he means is genuine, "outside" is a broad set of possibilities, but my understanding of where this is going is clear. He's going to yell at me.

"Are you outside of the Merchandise Mart?" I ask.

"What the fuck is the Merchandise Mart?" he asks.

"It's in Chicago," I say. "Are you looking for the New York office, maybe?"

"I'm not looking for it, I'm standing outside of it," he says.

I ask if he has the name of someone I could transfer him to. He says "Jesus Christ" and hangs up.

He calls again, and we repeat our performance. I ask again if he has the name of someone I could transfer him to, and he says, "Look, this is Tom Jordan, I'm just trying to get in." He still won't tell me if he's in New York or if he's in Chicago, but I know he's in New York. I tell him that I'm in Chicago but that I'm happy to transfer him to the New York office line, and he has a little more verve and says "Can anybody in this shithole let me in?" and I say "Maybe, just one—" and he sighs and hangs up.

While waiting for the steamboat of time or whatever to lurch me forward unto my death, I google "Tom Jordan" and learn he's one of the showroom's top designers. I find an unsurprising portrait on his website. I look at his sweater, at his pink face, at the restaurant-grade Twombly knockoff behind him in his summer home, his smug gaze, stack of magazines on his coffee table, legs crossed at the ankle like a proper Edwardian lass, and I imagine a violent home invasion. His gasping, girlish shouts.

I fold my hands in my lap and re-create him in my mind, ordering his underwear online (Barneys), bringing a picture of a cool haircut to the salon, his young girlfriend's jaw setting compulsively when she smells his breath, his dog's apathy when he walks in the door, his father's dying words (*I wish you had been less of a dick*), a group of high school kids mocking his outfit, him throwing away his new glasses, that vest, hand tailored, even though it had all looked so cool the day before, pure Johnny Depp, all the times people had put up with him for his money, his jokes and his advances tolerated with tight smiles, no one to confide in but nothing to confide, spending a little extra to get the teak on the boat, to impress who, though, I ask, his fortunes flagging, suddenly everyone yelling at him, all the time, what the fuck, pooping more frequently than usual, wizened butt cheeks hiding behind $200 khakis, his ulcer growing, wondering which of all these fuckers is going to fuck with him next, and pre-emptively fucking with anyone anonymous and servile, not taking into account that maybe, somehow, psychically I— we, together—by the power of wishing real hard or what-ever, are making his ulcer grow, the solidarity of our energy coming together to mess with his bod and its functions, like in that book *Thinner,* and it is with ease that I imagine his colleagues doing impressions of him when they're drunk at parties he's not invited to, rolling their eyes behind his back, nailing that lilt in his voice when he thinks he's being pro-found, and then my supervisor comes up behind me and asks if everything is okay.

The timing is enough to make me paranoid, I wasn't able to help Tom Jordan, *the* Tom Jordan, and now I'm going to get fired, oh well, so it goes.

I release my cheek from between my teeth and tell her, "Yeah, totally, what's up?"

She asks if she can see my junk mailers, or, formally, "welcome packets." I stand and walk to the copy room, show her the mailers. She opens them, judges my work. She's very slender and a few years younger than I am. It's easy to imagine her complaining about her neighbors and being uptight with waiters, the terse snort and widened downcast eyes when they interrupt her with the water pitcher.

She shuffles the papers and sighs, trying to make my job seem more important, so that her overseeing of my job can seem more important. I stand behind her, painfully uncertain of what to do with my hands, remembering being asked not to pee, Tom Jordan still in my system, watching her shake her head no, well, this isn't quite right, like any of it matters, talking to me but I can't hear her over the ringing in my ears. She seems to be showing me how to use a paper clip. She holds it in her hands, demonstrating both the right and the wrong way.

Holy absurdity, little side on top, big side on bottom, I guess I did it wrong. I say, "Oh, okay, that makes sense." "It's a matter of style," she explains. "I totally get it," I say, speaking in low tones, soothing and reassuring, nodding, and to keep the indignant scream from leaving my lips, I imagine that she needs to poop, all the time, but can't.

She asks me, "Do you think you're okay here now?"

I say, "Sure, of course, yeah."

"Any problems?"

"No, none that I can think of."

Neither of us, I guess, knows how to end this momentous and important tête-à-tête, so we stand there in the copy room for a second that, as they say, stretches, until she breaks and says "okay" and we both walk back to our desks.

I fix my packets, stare at the wall, and go home ten minutes before 5:00.

At home, I make brussels sprouts for dinner. They're covered in olive oil and likely too much vinegar, but the hissing sound, the fanfare of it all, sounds good. Real home cooking. I'm watching TV on the laptop for company, as usual, and I think about how much I don't really like TV. Don't really think of myself as a TV person. I imagine that one day I'll listen to music while I make dinner, an act that feels very healthy and stable when I think about it, but for now I still need the TV. I know that *Forensic Files* is propaganda for the Justice Department, like all of these crime shows are, and that they instill a weird deference to authority and a childish fear of the other, and that TV in general messes with your perception of time and influences your desires and gives you unattainable expectations for life, but I still can't make it through the night without it. It's okay for me to watch TV because I'm aware of what's really going on. I take it one step further, recognizing that that last idea is wrong. Recognition is not the first step to change. Not in my experience, anyway.

chapter 3

Karen thought, yeah sure, the new girl can talk, and she owns a skirt and knows how to use a computer, but there was something really not clicking about it, something a little off-putting about her.

She'd asked Millie not to stay until 5:30 (as originally planned) just so she could check her internet search history before closing the showroom. The search history was surprisingly normal. Household organizing tips, a few searches for designers that the showroom represented, recipes, low-cost clothing, news articles, a calculator.

The temp agency had said that Millie was one of their best workers, but the temp agency didn't really seem to understand that Lisa Hopper had an image to maintain, and that this was a social and creative position. That the applicant would need to be above and beyond. It was a two-month temp-to-perm job, but Karen knew she wouldn't be asking Millie to stay on.

When Millie walked up to Karen's desk each morning, just to give a monotone and strange hello, Karen wanted to say something about how it wasn't necessary to do that, but of course she couldn't, that would be rude, so Karen just widened her eyes a little, as if incredulous, nodded, said hello, and then her mind would turn to what it might take, budget-wise, to replace her quickly and efficiently.

For temp-to-hire positions, this particular agency took a half-up-front finder's fee for placements, which was refundable if there was an immediately obvious mismatch within the first seven days of employment, but Millie had been employed for twelve days, and Karen didn't notice that she'd missed the deadline until two days ago, which was already three days too late to get the money back (or to transfer it to another placement through the agency, which she would have been open to at first—and which actually made the arrangement seem risk-free when they entered into it, but which now seemed fucked up and annoying, because to be quite honest, if Millie was one of their best workers, she seriously questioned the agency's judgment).

Karen had a meeting planned with Lisa, the CEO, who would be in town soon, and who she wanted to impress. Her plan, initially, was to impress Lisa by replacing Agnes, the niece of one of the designers, and Millie's predecessor. Agnes was in retrospect a good fit, but too chatty, too confident, and a little too young. She had abruptly quit with a face-scratchingly obnoxious resignation letter about how she had come to realize that she needed to pursue her dreams of becoming a textile designer in New York, and had accepted a slot in the MFA program at Pratt, and that she hoped to have the opportunity to work with Lisa Hopper again in the future—overly gracious, implying that when they saw her again she would be bigger and better than what she was now, bigger and better than what they all were now.

Everyone had been very impressed when Karen arranged for a replacement through a temp agency, and she was happy to be able to play it cool. It was easy to imagine becoming executive assistant within a few years, and then by the time she was forty, being in an even better position within the company—or a similar company.

She had a business administration degree from Kalamazoo College and had started at Lisa Hopper as an intern and worked her way up, and she had picked up a lot of the business on the job. She even decorated her own apartment using learned principles and was thinking about, after a few tweaks, submitting photos to Apartment Therapy. It would be nice if someone in the office accidentally discovered it online, and mentioned it, and she could play it off, but she was also open to the idea of going to Lisa directly and sharing the link. As long as she could figure out a way to do it where it didn't seem like she was angling to get a designer job, because she was more interested in running the showroom than she was in working with clients. Lisa was based in New York, but that only meant, even more, that she needed strong support here in Chicago.

Karen could go to Holly, the current executive assistant

in Chicago, to air her misgivings about Millie, but she really wanted to be able to phrase it properly and to present a few solutions.

Karen was looking into getting an intern from the Art Institute or Columbia, which would be free but would require site visits from the schools and extra paperwork, which Lisa and Holly might not be open to. The other problem with an intern would be that Karen couldn't ask them to come in for a forty-hour week, which was what was needed for the phones, but maybe they could find someone to intern over the winter break, just to buy time and make back the money they'd lost on the temp.

Karen had paid $1,500 up-front to place Millie, and they were paying the agency $20 hourly, which seemed high for someone to sit around and answer phones.

If they went down to, say, $15 an hour for the reception assistant, it would take just under a month to recoup the $1,500 finder's fee. Karen knew the art schools took longer winter breaks, so this could work out perfectly. Three weeks of an intern, during which time they could find a suitable replacement at $15 an hour.

The real problem was that she couldn't wait too long to present this idea to Lisa, but she didn't want to do it via email, and she probably should go through Holly to get things solidified sooner rather than later, so they didn't somehow get stuck, contractually, with adding Millie to payroll.

The best would be if she was a no-show, which would put her in violation of her contract.

Another option would be to say that the position was superfluous, and that Lisa could save money by having the calls routed to Karen's desk. But that would demean Karen's position and make it harder for her to move forward with special projects.

Holly came in and said hey, and Karen stood up and said hello.

Millie breezed in five minutes later, ten minutes late, and gave Karen a weird smile and wave, and when Millie said "hello" it sounded like a piece of phlegm got caught in her throat, and the second half of her greeting was silent, just "he—" and a mouthed "llo." Karen smiled and nodded, then looked down at her notebook. Wheels turning.

chapter 4

There's a nightmare familiarity every morning when I wake. The quality of the light, sort of grayish-dim, the stiff feeling of my body, the smell, part dirty clothing, part cooking oil, part garbage, part incense. I'm reminded of how afraid I am to die, and how every morning is just one more used-up day.

I lie in bed for twenty minutes, feeling this, then make myself coffee and get dressed, no shower. Soon enough, I'm on the train again, and the feeling has somewhat faded. It's been replaced with hostility.

I walk past Karen's desk, and I smile and wave and say hello, unable to differentiate this greeting from all of the other greetings from the past weeks.

There's a lot of repetition in my life. No real routine or narrative, just a lot of repetition, and before I know it, I'm sitting in the break room drinking a cup of coffee (it doesn't taste good) and staring at my phone again, scrolling, waiting for the motivation to get up and go to my desk.

I think I'm drawn to temp work for the slight atmospheric changes. The new offices and coworkers provide a nice illusion of variety. Like how people switch out their cats' wet food from Chicken and Liver to Sea Bass, but in the end, it's all just flavored anus.

Two of the designers are rehashing what I imagine is an old conversation. The taller of the two is talking about toxic friendships and friend breakups, when to ease out and when to draw the line. The shorter one nods and gives a choral "Yeah" from time to time.

They're complaining about how they don't have any time, so busy, too busy for bullshit. "I don't know, she's having major troubles right now, and she feels like her mom isn't respecting her choices or her boundaries, and her mom keeps meddling, and I'm sympathetic of course, but I'm just so sick of hearing about it, but obviously I can't tell her that directly, because that's excessively harsh, and I don't want to be an asshole."

Another "Yeah" followed by a "totally know what you mean."

"I'm in a place in my life where I want to be around people who have their shit together and people who are going to help me grow. I'm at my limit, and honestly if you can't stand up to your own mother, you probably aren't bringing that much to the table for me anyway."

The choral girl laughs and says, "Right?"

I note this woman's shape-shifting performance. How by saying a thing, she becomes it. As she complains about how boring it is to hear her friend complain about her mother, as she goes into detail, masterfully reenacting specific boring conversations (both between her and her friend, and her friend and her friend's mother), she is essentially becoming them both, becoming the boredom she claims to want to remove from her life and mind, but which have complete control of her, and she doesn't notice that by saying "I don't like this" over and over she is just drawing herself closer to it, essentially becoming her friend and subjecting us all to what she claims to hate.

I think this must be quite common, and I think this woman must be an idiot, and I think I should stand up and go to my desk, but I stay here, thinking about this woman's friend's mother, and how, despite this woman using words that indicate she has spent time researching relationships on the internet (primary friend, boundaries, toxic, etc.), she seems to have no grasp of what is going on in her own mind, and how her thoughts and actions are affecting her experiences and, likely, her relationships.

My stomach growls, and I decide that maybe she is aware but can't help herself. There are things we all know we shouldn't do but do regardless. She might think that venting will help her find the relief and clarity she needs to move forward toward some lame ideal.

I must be glaring, because, out of the corner of my eye, I see Karen looking at me. She's mixing her yogurt with a spoon and doesn't break eye contact when I glance over. I'm startled, and I stand too fast and knock over the plastic chair, and I say, "Oh my gosh!"

Half of the women ignore me, but some of them smile,

and one of them says, "Ugh, fuck these chairs." And then they all talk about the chairs and how much they hate them. I right the chair and apologize, smiling, charmingly shy. I apologize again and it goes unacknowledged, except for by Karen, who says, with no warmth, that it's okay.

I put my headphones in my coat pocket in the coat closet, and I can feel the crumbs lining my pockets, not to paint myself too pathetically. There are certain circumstances where that would be preferable. Crumbs in the pockets used to be a statement, if I recall, about my nonconformity. Yes, and how perfectly all those decisions worked out for me. How blissfully free and *off the grid* or whatever I am.

I open up my email, see that I have three unread messages, and go through the normal emotional fanfare, thinking in rapid flashes something like "you're going to prison" or "you're going to die" or "everybody hates you."

The band of my skirt cuts into my empty gut. I listen to two designers talk about pedometers, and my palms become wet.

After all that drama, the contents are almost a disappointment. I am eligible for a mild discount at the Container Store, among other things.

When the phone rings, I jump. I attempt to transfer the call and wait for the person to call back and tell me it didn't work.

It should be easier to feel good.

I open an incognito window and do some research and learn that what makes most people happy is to be in touch with friends and family.

I used to have a boyfriend, James, who came as a

package-set with a nice, respectable gaggle of buddies, who I hated. There was some kind of burbling, unaddressed hostility coursing through me in those days (oh how the times have changed). I admit that I was occasionally rude to his friends, occasionally I was a little *too much* (his words) at home and in public. Maybe a little self-centered. Back then, a sense of something more—like *Oh, there must be something more!*—was always nagging at me, like I was waiting, like my situation and my relationships were unimportant because of their seeming transience.

I text my friend Sarah to see if she'd like to get a drink.

I hear one of the designers talking to a client on the phone, trying to schedule something. There's a lot of bold laughter, loud friendly sentences. She is presenting herself as a mixture of accommodating ("Well, that's completely up to you, Linda") and urgent ("Let's not wait too much longer on the Emery order, shipping takes forever"). I anticipate a dramatic sigh, possibly a "Jesus Christ," when she hangs up.

chapter 5

Sarah and I met at a house party two months after James and I broke up and three months after my job as a glorified spell-checker at the Art Institute ended on "mutual terms." She talks too much, almost constantly, needlessly repeating herself. Sometimes I try to interject, but it's useless. She thinks I don't hear her, or she knows I hear her but thinks my reactions are inadequate, so she tries a second time, saying the same phrase again, but faster or louder, which is something I do, too, when I'm drunk or bored, which I guess she often is when she's around me.

I'm a very good judge of character, I think. Sometimes it takes two encounters, because my mood shifts, or other people's moods shift, but I knew who Sarah was, despite her attempts to guide me, from our first meeting. She told me she didn't like drama and confrontation, which was an obvious tell, a "red flag" if you care about shit like that, which

usually I don't. I knew that if I tacitly allowed her to dominate the conversation, it would addict her to my company
and lead her to flatter me by texting me and contacting me
frequently, which would make me feel safe, an insider to a
small group. It was perfect for both of us, I imagine. What
I was looking for at the time we met was anyone, any body,
to fill my time on nights and weekends.

These days, I'm finding our dynamic very boring, and as
I walk to the bar to meet her, with all these thoughts on my
mind, the past, the present, all the decisions I've made, all
the decisions that have been made for me, I'm finding it hard
to conjure social excitement.

To keep my thoughts from coming, I think, *Oh, whatever,* as loud as I can, three times, and shake my head and
shoulders.

I get to the bar, and Sarah is there.

I say, "Hey, how's it going?"

She doesn't stand up and give me a hug or anything, just
puts her phone down and says, "Hey."

She runs her hands through her hair and sighs, acting
self-important, playing a part, the hard worker, defeated by
circumstance, a gentle soul misunderstood in the hard
world. I know I'm about to hear some long-winded tale
about how hard it is to work a real full-time job.

We order the special. It's a "mystery beer" with a shot of
"mystery whiskey." The bartender calls us girls. There's a
plaque behind the bar that reads "How much madder could
your wife get? HAVE ANOTHER BEER."

We sit back down at our table, and I say, "Cheers," and
then, "How was your day?"

Sarah says, "Just fucking ridiculous."

Her boss is making her send out a newsletter that inadvertently sexualizes a teen from their after-school program. The boss won't listen to Sarah's well-reasoned pitches for altering the text, all is doomed, and the anecdote blossoms and unfolds into a company-wide conspiracy where Sarah is the central victim. It's boring, a long one, so I'm shaky on the details.

"Wow," I say.

"I mean, it's whatever," says Sarah. "Do you want another beer?"

"Yeah, sure," I say.

"You can get the next round," she says. I nod.

She returns with the beers, and I ask, to punish myself by prolonging the topic, "Did you get your boss to change the newsletter?"

"No," says Sarah.

"That's a bummer," I say.

"Yeah, it's fine. My name isn't on it. This is just what she does, though, she's completely clueless."

I feel myself winding up to give her deflating advice. My forte.

"Can you go to HR? It seems like there are a lot of things going on in your office that are inappropriate."

She has one of her easily interpretable facial spasms. My advice has offended her, as usual.

"Yeah, I really don't know what good that would do," she says.

"Maybe just having it on record would make you feel like you had more control of the situation. If enough people went to HR . . ."

This time it's the lip. The fishhook of disgust. Her eyes fix on a spot above my head. "I don't know, I'll figure it out. It's just really stressful."

I turn the conversation to my job, where things are less operatic but very likely more depressing. I tell her that I feel like my life is completely meaningless and empty.

"Yeah, okay," she says.

"I'm supposed to answer the phones, but they basically never ring. And I have to paper-clip these papers in this particular way. And the people there, oh my god." I recount the conversation I overheard about the girl who was complaining about her friend complaining about her mother, and I try to articulate what was interesting to me about it. I tell her about the bathroom breaks thing.

"Yeah, you told me that already," she says, as if she never repeats herself. As if I'm the one who's boring. Maybe if I'd used more hand gestures and smiled at her, she would have found it funny.

"Oh, sorry. It's just a really boring job. I feel really extraneous and insecure."

"Yeah, well, it's not forever," she says. I wince, knowing that there's some falseness in that statement, knowing that if it's not this job, it'll be the next.

Sarah asks if I'm being assertive and describes three occasions where she was assertive as a temp, and how each occasion led to an offer of permanent employment.

I nod throughout her advice and say, "You're right, I could be more assertive. I just don't want to be annoying."

"It's not annoying to ask to take on more. It's worse if they think you're lazy or incompetent."

"Yeah, I guess you're right," I say.

We finish our beers, go out front for a smoke, and then I order another round of specials.

She talks more about her job, I nod, I finish my shot, it helps. I ask her if she's thinking about quitting her job, hoping it might lead to us quitting this conversation. She says she can't afford to. I raise my eyebrows and nod.

I ask her if she's seen a movie I just watched, and then I describe the movie to her. She says no and asks me if I've seen a TV show she likes. I say no, and she describes an episode to me. I try to flatter her by saying that the movie, the one I referenced earlier, is very intellectual and dense, and that's why she might like it.

"Oh, okay, that sounds cool, but I haven't seen it." She seems annoyed, and then I feel annoyed, and then I order another round.

I don't really remember how the night wrapped up, but I remember trying to put my keys on the hook by the door and tripping when I took my boots off. I'd read earlier that having a nightly ritual can help pull you out of a fog, and I lament not having the stamina to brush my teeth and put on night cream before making tea and reading, maybe rubbing lavender oil on my scalp to help me have nice dreams. I drink some water in the kitchen and have a punishingly nostalgic memory of James.

It's 9:30 when I get in bed.

chapter 6

Kristin was lying on her back on the couch, staring up at the ceiling, reflecting idly on her day. She'd been partnered with Lindsey on a long project. It was fine. It would be fine. Lindsey had some concentration issues and a tendency to hijack the conversation and bring it around to her personal life, which seemed constantly frustrated. Today it was some issue Lindsey was having with her friend, because Lindsey's friend's mother wasn't respecting her friend's autonomy, and Lindsey was annoyed with her friend for venting about it so often. Whenever Kristin tried to redirect the conversation back to work, Lindsey would roll her eyes and say "Okaaayyy" and then pout for an hour. "I feel like a hostage negotiator!" was something Kristin imagined she might one day say.

Kristin had just learned that she could reverse the direction of her ceiling fan, and that if she did that, it would serve a different purpose. Clockwise, the fan cooled the room. Counterclockwise, it circulated air and kept the apartment fresh. Something about the angle of the fan blades.

Kristin tried to empty her mind. She watched how the blades of the fan strobed the overhead light. She tried to follow one of the blades with her eyes. She looked beyond the blades to the crack in the plaster on her ceiling. As her mind cleared, she got a tart feeling in her chest. She couldn't identify its specific cause, but it was very strong. It wasn't exactly a sad feeling, because sadness was more often located in the stomach—this was right at the base of the rib cage, stinging and tart. Its underlying texture was a feeling of connection with something larger, but since Kristin was clearing her mind, and just letting her body speak, she didn't try to pin down the feeling with language or with an internal inventory of possible sources.

Ever since Kristin had started meditating, twenty minutes every morning, she got these sensations. Sometimes it felt like static when it happened in her face or hands, but when it was in her chest or solar plexus it felt bittersweet, tart, stinging. She didn't know if these sensations were coming from within her—maybe some unaddressed melancholy she'd been carrying around—or if these feelings were being picked up from the atmosphere. Like maybe the meditation had unlocked level-5 empathy receptors in her brain, and as she moved through her day, grazing her hand along the banister up to the train platform, running her fingers along the fax machine panel at work, taking her coffee from the barista, edging through crowds on the sidewalk, she was picking up on some kind of collective, gentle human loneliness. The sensations weren't bad. They were, at times, a bit sumptuous even. It was a new feeling. She'd thought the meditation would clear and calm her mind, which would help her focus on problem solving at work, but then, she reflected, on the couch, still in her work clothes, that she was a pretty even-minded person to start with—conflict averse, flexible in terms of perspective, not shy about taking responsibility for her errors, open and sympathetic even with difficult people—so, maybe what meditation did to a mind like hers was to open it up a bit, to let in other feelings, to give her some kind of larger perspective on humanity that others didn't have.

And though she liked these feelings, she preferred to keep them private, as she thought of herself as a practical and pragmatic person on the whole. She'd mentioned her meditation practice to her friends but had withheld these side effects and simply told them that it had helped with her headaches and her diet, which, of course, was also true.

chapter 7

I wake up ill. I feel trapped in a loop. I stare at the big pile of clothing on the floor. I eat some dry cereal. I wash my armpits. I go to work. I think things on the train. I ride the elevator. I walk to Karen's desk. I am either calm or hollow, hard to say. I ask, "Is there anything extra I can do today? The phones have been pretty quiet, and I finished those packets."

Karen seems caught off guard. "Well, you can make more packets. We really need you by the phones. I'll try to think of something for you if you're bored, but I'm just trying to finish up all this work I have here." She gestures to a slim notebook.

"Oh, okay, great!" My voice is weak. "I'm not bored, I just want to be helpful."

As I walk through the showroom, I recognize my gamble. I make $12 an hour, the best-paying job I've had in more than a year. If I'm making twelve, they're paying the agency at least fifteen, up to twenty, so in the middle let's say eighteen, times thirty-five is $630 a week, times two weeks is $1,260, times two is more than $2,500 a month to have me, the idiot, sit in a chair, doing about four hours of work a week, sixteen hours of work a month, which puts the rate for my actual services at around $150 an hour.

I see a big brown vase shaped like a jug, rudimentary, meant to evoke some kind of tribal thing, filled with dried stems, sitting on a metal sideboard. If I could compress and stretch time at will, at $150 an hour, I could buy that jug just to make fun of it. At $150 an hour, I could probably even dress seductively enough to make new friends.

No donuts in the break room today, just stale bread, which I eat with gusto.

I say "Good morning" to one of the designers. She must think I'm talking to someone else, and that's fine.

I liberate some bread from behind my right upper molar, and I realize I might still be a little drunk. I walk to my desk.

I turn on my computer and the phone rings, another angry person in the middle of a project that gives them the illusion of progress. I transfer her to the textiles department. She calls back and tells me there was no one in the textiles department. She seems very angry and asks if I could please connect her to an actual person. I apologize, a scream trapped in my chest, and say I'll try someone else. She calls back, and when she hears it's me, she sighs, mutters, and hangs up.

I wonder what it would be like if I handled things

differently. I wonder what would have happened, when the woman called back, if I had said, "Jesus fucking Christ, are you fucking kidding me? I'm sorry, there's supposed to be someone in the textiles department at all times. This keeps happening, I'm so sorry. We're trying to run a business here, and it's impossible to run a business when you have all these girls running around playacting like they own the place. Hold one second, I'm going to get someone on the phone for you. This is unacceptable."

Would she have liked that? Would that have affirmed her set of life principles? If I had done that, would I have had the courage to use the PA system? Maybe you can change the way you feel by trying out new personalities. I meditate on this.

The designers in the office mill around, not chained to their desks like I am. I look at them, wondering who I should approach first. Today, I will find some work to do. I will be assertive.

Fear keeps me in my seat.

I check my email for any life-changing news. I've been sent another newsletter from the women's shelter.

I volunteered there for two weeks last year as part of a misguided emotional remodeling. The job was frightening and difficult but also very boring, and I must have known I hated it because I overslept one day and woke around noon to five missed calls from the shelter, which I did not return, and they emailed me daily for a week or so, desperate, but I never checked the emails, and I never went back, and I tried to forget I'd ever done it, and I never mentioned it, except for one time at a bar with Sarah, trying to impress a stranger with my worldliness and sophistication, I said, "Well, I actually volunteer at a women's shelter, so . . ."

I'm too humiliated to open the shelter's newsletters to unsubscribe. They go out twice a month. A weird reminder of my failures.

The other email is from Credit Karma letting me know there have been some developments with my credit score, which, oh, who cares, *what a plebian trifle.*

I get up and think about my body as a tentative, vulnerable thing, clasping my hands in front of my crotch, and I try to act out "peeking" around the cubicle wall behind my desk. I knock on the corner of the wall and say, "Hey, I'm the new reception temp. The phones have been quiet, and I have extra time if there's any busywork I can help you with."

This woman has never registered before. She's an actual adult, mid-forties with grayless shiny red-brown hair and thick baubles around her neck.

She says, "Oh no, sweetie, we're all good here."

I'm a thirty-year-old woman, and I smell like an onion pizza. I say, "Okay, let me know!"

Back at my desk I sit and slowly collect money that I can use to pay the rent on my apartment and on food so that I can continue to live and continue to come to this room and sit at this desk and slowly collect money.

More time passes, and I watch a subtitled video about an AI robot named Sonja who wants to help out in hospitals and in customer service and hopes to have a house and family someday, and I think, *Yeah, right, Sonja.*

The phone rings, I transfer the call. I sit. I make a gesture toward assembling a few packets. Karen comes to my desk, and I fear the worst. I turn to her in my swivel chair, my armpits wet with sweat, and I can feel how dry my lips and face are, how ridiculous I must look, how hungry I am from only having stale bread and dry cereal all day. I think she's going to fire me. I'm not so much bracing for it as I am having a kind of paroxysm, adrenaline filling me up, and a loud, deep voice shouting *yeah well fuck you too* in my ears.

"So, I have some extra work for you," she says.

"Oh, fantastic!" I say, really believing it to be fantastic in the moment. My expectations so fucked up that my relief at having more clerical work is real and strong.

Karen doesn't smile, doesn't react, maybe there's a micro-flinch there like she thinks I'm a loser for being excited to do whatever it is she's about to make me do.

"Come with me," she says.

I stand to follow her, nervously eyeing the phone I'm about to leave. If it rings in front of her, I'll pounce on it and maybe impress her with my agility and dedication, my ability to multitask.

In the copy room, she bends down and brings out a small document shredder and pushes it toward me with her foot. She looks at me like I know what this means, like she's just shown me the lord's chamber pot and I'm supposed to understand.

I push the thing back to my desk like it's a tiny shopping cart, hands on both sides, and wait for her. She comes back with a ridiculously small stack of papers. I try not to interpret it too much.

"I went around and collected these papers from everyone in the office. Do you know how to work a shredder?" she asks.

"Oh, yeah, I've done a ton of shredding. I shredded a whole file room's worth of documents at my last job," I say, dying to impress. "This'll be really quick."

"Well, there's no pressure to get it finished by the end of the day. Prioritize the phones, and let me know if you have any questions."

"Sure, thanks," I say. "And let me know if there's anything I can do from my computer, if you need any filing done, or if there's any other busywork that people need help with. I'm happy to multitask."

She doesn't react, she barely nods, and she tells me again to let her know if I have any questions.

I plug the shredder in and feed it a stack of about twelve papers. I pause, then put a few sheets in singly.

I get a few more calls. I text Sarah to let her know that the scheme worked, that I have been given an extra task. On impulse, I include the small image of the lightning bolt, the rainbow, and the most pathetic-looking face I can find. The worried one. It makes me feel old and uncomfortable. Sarah responds "nice" and includes the lightning bolt and a baby chick. We text a moment longer.

I put another piece of paper into the shredder and watch it jerk around before it disappears.

Most of the documents are copies of checks, invoices, credit card numbers. None of this interests me. I pause when I see the word *shit* on one of the documents. It's a printed-out email, containing rich "I feel" language, exclamation points, heated opinions. For some reason, I don't feel comfortable shredding it. There's something dear about it. I put it in my notebook when no one is looking (no one is ever looking).

The hours pass.

I leave the majority of the shredding for tomorrow, even though I could have easily finished it in about fifteen minutes.

At the end of the day, I put my notebook in my bag, shut off my computer, and leave.

Karen was hoping that giving her an extra task would keep Millie out of her hair while she arranged for her replacement. She'd chosen the documents randomly out of a file in the back room marked "Shred."

chapter 8

My building is so quiet that I have, a few times, thought I was the only one living in it, even though there are about sixteen units. I put my coat on the chair and hear footsteps coming up the stairs and I freeze.

The footsteps stop. I hear a door open and shut, and I take off my boots.

I turn on *Forensic Files*, and it seems like they have a new writer. I light a cigarette, not in the mood to eat yet. The narrator keeps saying "cut to the chase." The detectives cut to the chase, asking Angelo if he'd seen Lydia on the day of her murder. When Dr. Andrews was called in to take his polygraph, detectives cut to the chase, asking him if he had killed the little girl in Plaintown, Indiana. I walk through the apartment and turn on a few lamps. My preference is for dimmer light, somewhere between 40- and 60-watt bulbs and yellowish shades. Cozy.

I cry for a second, but I'm faking it. Waaaaaaahhhhhh. Poor me, poor me, who cares. This is what I wanted. To sit here and not have someone judging me. I'm fat, I smell, no one likes me, my clothes suck, I'll never amount to anything, everyone around me is an idiot, self-involved, judgmental, stupid, too dumb to know the harm they're doing, too dumb to know they're not happy inside, not like me, I know. Ha-ha-ha.

I was right about it all, being alone is clarifying. And there I go, I'm crying again, but still faking it, half of me still unmoved.

I open my bag to take out the email I stole from the office. There's a voided check in my notebook, too, an accident—whoops! I put the check on my refrigerator. I stare at the Chococat magnet's mouthless face and wide eyes like a Mesopotamian idol hovering above the routing number. Longest eye contact I've made all month.

I find some old cheese and the stale butt of a baguette and eat this (dinner) at my table in front of my show. The victim's mom says something like "I guess that was Lydia's purpose in life. To get this man off the streets." This is played over home footage of Lydia, eight years old, riding a pink bike in a driveway.

I usually don't feel anything with these shows, and I don't particularly feel anything now, but this statement makes me think.

I wonder if it's a misunderstanding of life to look for purpose, or if the mom, then, following through, thinks that her purpose—the full sum of her own life—was to give birth to a girl who would get the sweater fibers of a child rapist under her fingernails. I selfishly and halfheartedly think about my own life's purpose, then shift to thinking about Lydia, the girl, and what it would be like if she hadn't been attacked and killed. Would she be sitting in her apartment thinking, idly, about the purpose of her life, until she met someone and had a child who would eventually sit, alone, in their apartment wondering, idly, about the purpose of their life? I'm annoyed by the mother's need to find a positive spin.

Sometimes I pretend I'm feeling vengeful for the murder of someone I love. I play through the scenario, trying to make myself weep. I try to imagine what it would be like to be in favor of capital punishment, but I can't. I'm indifferent to punishment.

I hear the front door of my building open and footsteps coming up the stairs again. I mute my laptop and look for incense, empty my ashtray, and open the window, in case it's my landlord coming to discuss some kind of problem he has with me.

I want to take a shower, get nice and clean, but I don't.

I remove my disgusting clothing and get into bed, bringing the laptop with me, hoping to fall asleep quickly because I really have nothing good to think about. I'm a little annoyed that I'm thinking about James again, and I blame Sarah for it, somehow. James used to say I was good at being ugly and indiscriminately resentful, and maybe that's what I'm doing now. And maybe he liked my resentful side, and that's why he said I was good at it. Who knows!

I'm glad he's gone. He had a talent for making me feel mean. We dated for four years, lived together for three of them, happily for two. Sometimes I can still feel him in the other room, judging me, avoiding me. Sometimes I still have the impulse to throw off the sheets and storm out into the living room, grab him by the elbow, and, in a voice even I admit is frightening, say, *"I know you're out here judging me, you dumbass piece of shit."*

I'm angry now. I get out of bed to go smoke in the kitchen, and I notice that my hand is shaking. It's embarrassing, mostly, to think of the way I used to behave. I put out my cigarette, brush my teeth, get back in bed, and unpause my episode.

I'm only half paying attention. Another person with a bad idea about how to get out of an uncomfortable situation. Another attempt at a violent shortcut to a fantasy life. I slip in and out of the narrative until, eventually, sleep overtakes me.

chapter 9

Work again, another fucking waking nightmare.
Karen walks by my desk and glances down at the
pile of unshredded paper. I thought this was what she
wanted. But of course not, it was, as usual, some kind of a
test and I did not pass. She said to take my time. She wanted
to think I was incompetent, so wasn't I giving her what she
wanted, and wasn't that very gracious of me in a way?

The women around me make phone calls, talk lightly
with each other. The older woman walks by my desk and
says hello and I say hello and I smile, my spine curved, my
organs crushed.

I laugh a little bit at my desk. The kind of laugh where
your eyes water and your chin wrinkles and you feel like you
might throw up.

It's almost noon. I look over at the shredder. I find the

cord and hold it for a minute, staring at it, feeling time move through me.

I plug it in. I turn it on. I know that if I just complete the task I will feel better.

I want to go home.

But not to my apartment home, to my thirteen-years-ago home, to my hug-my-mother home, say I will make her proud, apologize, explain I can do better this time, be in my bed, be in my room, look at a magazine, plan my day, start not from scratch but just a little bit back, make different decisions, try to cultivate confidence, try not to coddle bad thoughts, be better, take the right things seriously, not say the things I said to James, try to hold on to a job, monitor my expectations earlier. Bring them way down.

I pick up a small stack of papers and shred them and the phone rings. "Good afternoon, Lisa Hopper, how may I direct your call? Sure, one moment."

I shred another single sheet of paper, and I can hear a woman in the background comically, angrily raise her voice over the sound of the shredder, like she hates me for shredding. I have a paranoid fantasy in which Karen has chosen shredding for me to further alienate me from the office. I let it pass. Shred another sheet.

I should read a book, I should make some friends, I should write some emails, I should go to the movies, I should get some exercise, I should unclench my muscles, I should get a hobby, I should buy a plant, I should call my exes, all of them, and ask them for advice, I should figure out why no one wants to be around me, I should start going to the same bar every night, become a regular, I should volunteer again, I should get a cat or a plant or some nice lotion or some Whitestrips, start using a laundry service, start taking myself both more and less seriously.

I hear the woman with the pedometer come up behind me and talk about taking a walk break. She has to get a certain amount of steps in per day. She wants to go on a mall-walk through the food court, a real zero-sum, I think, assuming she'll get some kind of dense wheat bagel from Au Bon Pain, my brain repeating the thought "a real zero-sum" over and over until I'm afraid I might say it out loud.

The pedometer woman swoops up for a high five with someone else, and I can smell her perfume, floral and acrid but socially correct.

The woman in the corner cubicle crosses to talk to the Tupperware girl about the new French bulldog she just bought from a breeder in Indiana. She wants to get a dog walker, but she thinks dog walkers are kind of "shady."

"It feels kind of creepy to give my keys to a stranger, like I'm going to have to get some kind of a medieval fortress board to put over my door at night so my dog walker doesn't come in and kill me, haha."

I have a series of quick thoughts.

"Or, like, it's weird, sometimes my bedroom is kind of messy because I have a lot of clothes, so do I have to get a maid just so I can have a dog walker? It's, like, if you do one thing, it turns out you have to do, like, ten other things."

"Yeah," says Tupperware.

I feel very far from this woman and her problems. I feel it as a kind of unfairness.

"Look, his name's Dylan," she says, I assume holding out her phone.

It feels unfair that even when I imagine that I am also being shown the dog photos, I know I wouldn't be able to say anything about them. I would just make a stifled, positive-sounding noise, or say something provocative about dog breeders, or laugh nervously. I feel this more, maybe, than the unfairness that I haven't made a real decision in more than a year—and here she is faced with ten.

This woman probably will not get a maid or a dog walker. The threat she perceives makes me angry in its frivolousness. I imagine the dog, caged for days on end, peeing in a corner, humping her boyfriend's leg, barking neurotically, turning her cute space into a nightmare for visitors, and I imagine her eventually giving the dog up to a new owner who will have to learn to deal with its emotional and behavioral issues.

Whereas in her mind, she breaks down and shells out for the walker and for the maid. She hesitates when handing the walker her keys. He's nineteen and seems too aloof about the whole thing. In her mind, one night, while she's asleep in her room, the front door opens. The misfit teen enters, well aware of which floorboards creak, well aware of the location of her iPad, her laptop, her Birkin, and later it's not so much the financial blow but the feeling of being intruded on that gets her. She tries to brush it off "What a shit guard dog haha!" but with the lawsuit with the dog walking app, her recurring nightmares, the $60,000+ losses, she has to give the dog up because he's too emblematic of her trauma.

Both of our fantasies end in the dog being given up.

Maybe it will work out, and we're both jumping to con-
clusions.

I listen to more conversations in the office, transfer a call.
I try to do more shredding, but my arm feels like it's made
of lead. I read the news, watch some captioned silent videos,
and then I go home. I sit at my kitchen table and google sug-
gestions for how to make your living space more functional
and how to deal with needy friends who dominate the conversation. I'm preparing myself for the weekend, which is
somehow upon us again.

chapter 10

The puppy was so cute, so cute, so cute. But she really couldn't get over how many other things were on her mind regarding the puppy. Elodie named the puppy Dylan because she thought it was such a cute name, but thought it might be weird if she eventually had kids and named one of them Dylan, but things changed, and maybe by the time she had kids she wouldn't like that name anymore anyway. It was always better to just go for what you were feeling in the moment.

Elodie was on her way to get drinks with her girlfriends and was really excited to show them pictures of Dylan, had already planned out how she was going to ask them if they wanted to see a picture of a really hot guy she was dating, and in her mind her friends all buckled over with laughter, saying things like "Fuck you" or "Oh my god, shut up" because that was really just her kind of sense of humor. But of course they would want to see the pictures of Dylan, and she would tell them that they should absolutely come over and see him sometime.

"We should go dog walking on Sundays!"

Something like that. Elodie was always prepared for all the different ways a conversation could go. Always an anecdote or a suggestion or an invitation on deck.

She would bring up the fact that she was looking for a dog walker and then ask about etiquette for that, like how clean does your apartment need to be? Do you need a maid? Please advise, ugh, that was business parlance, so funny. She was such a dork.

When she entered the bar, black walls, real candles, perfect mix between grungy and classy, she saw her friends at the bar already talking, already laughing, great to see them, slightly nervous, as usual, she went up to them and hugged them, and got out her phone and held it in her hand, and waited for the right moment to bring it all up, waited for the right moment for her fantasy to become a reality.

"Hey, do you guys want to see a picture of this hot guy I've been seeing?" she asked, and they smiled at her, silent, and she showed them the puppy, and they smiled again and said, "Oh he's so cute, I didn't know you got a puppy." And right as she was about to go into her anecdotes about him, about what his name was and what her life with him was like, another friend, Clarissa, always the star, went into a speech about what it was like when she got her first puppy, and then everyone started taking turns telling puppy stories, and when would it be Elodie's turn to talk about the maid and the dog walker? She was the one who brought it up, so it was unfair that everyone else got to talk about it, and she got angry and blurted out "I think I need a dog walker" and one of them said "Yeah, probably" and that was that, and that was awful. This was not how it was supposed to go. This was not how it was supposed to be. She ordered a drink and tried to think of herself as a piece of bamboo, flexible but strong, but it wasn't working and nothing was going the way she thought it would.

Down the street from the bar where Elodie was having her conniption, Jessica ate the last almond from her Tupperware and went to the fridge for carrots, hummus, and a block of cheese. Her roommate's cat, Pippi, was lying on top of the fridge in a little box. Pippi stretched out her paw and Jessica put her finger on the soft pad, and Pippi curled her (de-clawed) fingers around it.

Jessica's roommate was in her bedroom watching a movie with her boyfriend. Jessica was doing the same, but on the couch, alone. She set the snacks on the coffee table and went back to the kitchen for an apple, a bag of kettle corn, and the almond milk ice cream. She'd turned down an offer to go out to a bar and was feeling an intense sense of control. She hit the bowl, blew the weed smoke out, and hit play. She was going to eat all the snacks. This was a choice. This was a no-pressure evening. All fucking week she'd been processing invoices and transferring data from the old system to Design Smart, watching tutorials online but fucking it up anyway. She'd told Holly it would take a few weeks, and Holly had given her that managerial look of disappointment, so she said she could have it done by next Wednesday.

What-fucking-ever, no more work thoughts. She was alternating between popcorn and ice cream. She'd specifically chosen this movie to watch because she'd seen it before. There was no room for new information in her mind. She loved—on the list of things she loved, this would be near the top—being in sweats, under a blanket, mildly stoned with a snack buffet in front of her. When her snippy aunt made anti-drug comments at family functions, she wanted to mind meld the aunt into this feeling to show her how wholesome it was. How marijuana could be a nice, medicinal way to get in touch with yourself, if you set parameters and expectations for the session. She ate an unwashed carrot straight from the bag and didn't laugh at a joke in the movie, even though she acknowledged that it was conceptually funny.

Jessica repeated to herself that she didn't feel guilty for skipping out on her friends to stay home, get high, and eat with abandon. This was a conscious choice she was making, not some weird antisocial reaction to stress and pressure.

After a while, she stopped thinking, and started watching the movie and feeling the bliss of chewing. She recognized new patterns. Things she hadn't noticed before. She let all her thoughts go and let herself sink into the present moment, which ultimately would help her engage more deeply in her weekly routine. She thought, briefly, of trying the new Keratin hair treatment tonight but wondered if it would be distracting or uncomfortable to have a plastic bag on her head for an hour.

chapter 11

Sarah invites me out to a party, a rare act of graciousness and inclusion and likely one of my three annual social outings. I go with the same intentions as most—to find a person who might realize, through a sympathy of dialogue, that I am the person they've been looking for to fulfill what's been missing in their emotional and intellectual lives.

As we walk to the party (we had a few drinks beforehand) Sarah tells me more about her job. I ask questions at the appropriate times, hoping she might ask me a question in return.

It's cold outside, and Sarah's coat and outfit, as usual, are better than mine, which at one point would have made me proud, would have meant I wasn't vain, but I get it better now. It's another failure of mine.

I hear myself say, "Jesus, that sucks," and Sarah seems irritated and says that it's fine.

I say, "You shouldn't have to put up with that, you should have a job where people treat you with *respect*," hoping she will respond to the notion of respect, but she doesn't respond at all, so I become prescriptive, walking the line between camaraderie and aggressive condescension, and say, "You should quit."

"I really can't afford to quit right now."

"Can you afford to not quit? I mean, in the long run? It might be good to have some fire under your feet."

"Oh, you think that's a good idea?" she says.

I think "yeah" but say, "No, I get it."

"I'm exhausted when I get home, and I can't afford to leave this job right now. Not everyone can afford to just do that."

This is, I assume, some allusion to her idea of my parents and my financial situation, since I'm able to have such shitty intermittent employment and still live in an apartment on my own.

We arrive, and I get a hug when I come in, because the hostess doesn't know me yet.

As I'm getting my hug Sarah says, "Millie really hates hugs," and laughs, and the hostess laughs and apologizes and says, "Yeah, my family wasn't all that into hugs either, I get you."

I hope we're not about to start talking about my fucking family and I say, "Oh, I don't mind," angry for talking about hugs as soon as we get to the party like I'm some child with boundary issues, daring Sarah to say one word about my family—but of course she won't.

"No, it's cool, it's cool," says the hostess, and I have no idea how to respond, racking my brain for something to say about hugs, some anecdote, something about science and hugs, almost going in for a second one to prove myself. My mind goes to bonobos, to a time when my estranged, effete cousin kissed me hello on the cheek and I recoiled and was haunted by it for months, to my extreme discomfort at having my hair braided by girls in grade school, to how Sarah and I have never hugged, even when she seems distressed, but I stalled too long, and the hostess asks Sarah how she is, and Sarah says things are fucked up at work, and I watch the ease with which the hostess relates with an anecdote about how her coworkers are a drag. She laughs, and I think it must be nice to project such happiness. I look for a crack to see what's really underneath, and I can't tell—probably a screeching loneliness, a safe bet. I make a straight line to the kitchen for a beer without excusing myself, and when I come back to the doorway, both are gone.

I have to find Sarah, because it feels too threatening to just go randomly up to a small, strange group of people and start talking.

I find her. She's reminiscing about a friend she used to have before she had me. There's a guy there talking to her, a guy she might be interested in sexually, but I don't know. We don't talk about those things. I stand there. No one introduces themselves. The assumption must be that I know everyone and everyone knows me, and sure that's a comfort, a minor one, but I take it, kicking back quite literally on my heels, smiling uselessly.

"Well, Kelly used to be really unhappy here, so I don't know."

"Yeah, but I think she's way more active in LA."

"Yeah, I'm not really sure what she's up to, but . . ."

The guy is not handsome, but I still want his attention. I want someone's attention. No one is looking at me. I rock on my heels. I almost whistle. To pass the time, I critique the decor. I think they have too many DVDs.

The guy looks over Sarah's shoulder and says "Uh-huh" while Sarah lists facts about their mutual friend who now lives in LA. He's bored. She's boring. I feel bored, and then I feel annoyed, and I wonder why no one ever wants to talk to me, because I'm a great conversationalist, it just takes me a minute to get into it. But once I get into it, I really roll, and things are really great. I remember a lot of times that I've been downright charming. I also remember a few times I've been abruptly aggressive, sure, but it's unhealthy to dwell on the past.

He's shifting on his feet. We're losing him. Someone has to intervene, and it has to be me. If nobody puts a stop to this, Sarah could keep going for hours, telling us, in different ways, over and over, that Kelly (whoever that is) has a job now in California.

Sarah pauses to breathe, and I take my opportunity. I hold out my hand.

"Hey, I'm Millie."

"Oh, hey, I'm [whatever]."

"How's it going?"

I'm starting from scratch, and I can tell Sarah is a little taken aback, but I truly doubt, in all honesty, that she can really be that taken aback because it's not like this was some kind of deep, interesting conversation I've just interrupted, and it was rude of her not to introduce me in the first place.

Sarah gives me a dirty look, too dirty for the offense.

There always seems to be this unspoken idea that if I start talking, something bad is going to happen. Like I'm going to take something too far or say something mean or weird. But the things I say are completely normal for the most part, and I think everyone is blowing everything out of proportion, like when my parents, on silent drives home from family functions, would critique my innocuous nine-year-old barbs, or when my dorm roommate took me aside and told me I needed to apologize for embarrassing our friend with some blithe comment, or when people's faces go cold when I talk when I'm in a good mood, or when James said "Wow, you really go for the jugular" just because I maybe got a little fed up with his friend Emily, the grad student, who always treated me like I was stupid, and one night, yes, a few drinks in, I laughed when she said "utilize" and she said "what?" and I said "just utilize, it's a meaningless word" and then she tried to tell me that it "communicated" something different from the word "use" and the way she looked at me, chuckling, glancing over at James like "oh, how sweet, it tried to talk," made me so mad that I might have said, maybe, something along the lines of "yeah, it communicates something, it's a real first-gen-college-grad kind of word, like your parents are small-town conservative Christians who didn't have any books in the house, and you're self-conscious about your upbringing so you want to stand out by using elitist intellectual language, but you don't actually know any long words, so you just truss up the word 'use' for no fucking reason other than to try to make people feel like you're the one with the big mental dick, even though 'utilize' is basically just administrative jargon and completely déclassé to them that knows."

All the heel nipping, all the corrections, all the hand-wringing when I open my mouth like something bad is going to happen, but honestly I can be very charming when the situation is right. I've only acted out a few times, and everyone makes mistakes.

On the walk home from that party, James told me that Emily's family was poor—hesitated to say "uneducated," but got it out eventually. "It was kind of fucked up what you said." "Well, I wasn't wrong, then," I said, humiliated by my impulse to humiliate. "No, you were really wrong. That was really wrong."

But I'm not at that party, I'm at this party, so I look up and say, "How was your day?" You see, it's charming, because it's something you would ask a boyfriend or close friend or a roommate or your child, but he and I don't know each other, so the contrast points to the general situation of us being strangers.

"I'm gonna get a beer," says Sarah, and fine, she should, she looks like she needs one. I try the thing that the hostess did and I smile, making sure my teeth are showing, and laugh a little bit and say, "Oh, could you get me one too?" because that would be what I would say if I were comfortable in the situation and comfortable with our friendship, which of course, haha, I am.

"Oh, uhh, my day was pretty good," he says. "Pretty normal."

"What does that look like for you?" I ask, as if wearing a ball gown, host of the party myself. "A normal day?"

"Went to work, got home, ate, came here."

"Pretty normal," I say, because sometimes it's correct to repeat what you've heard. "Same here, I guess," I say, really making an effort but wondering how soon Sarah will be back. "Where do you work?" I ask, putting my money where my mouth is.

"Downtown," he says, which I find surprising because he's dressed like a complete slob and has stray blond neck hairs jutting out in all directions, in small tufts, like he dry shaved five days ago with a single-blade disposable razor, eyes closed, distracted by how much he must love himself.

"Oh, cool, me too," I say, which is followed by a frightful pause, so I parry. "Or maybe it's not cool. I don't like my downtown job very much." I smile again. Maybe this is something we have in common.

"No, it's fine," he says.

I can feel Sarah approach me from behind and I almost shout, "Well, so do you like movies?" wondering what his fucking problem is.

"Yeah, sure."

"You like James Dean movies?" I say.

"I don't know," he says.

"*On the Waterfront*," I say.

"Sure," he says.

"What's the last movie you saw?" It's like sucking on a rock and pretending it's candy, talking to this guy.

"I don't actually watch movies that much," he says, nodding at Sarah.

"Oh, okay, cool," I say. "That's fine. That's your right."

Feigning enthusiasm about something and getting shot down. Looping memories keeping me out of the moment. He walks away.

Sarah slaps herself on the face to mean let's have a cigarette. I nod and follow her to the enclosed porch off the kitchen where people are smoking in their coats.

If people would just give an inch, I think they would realize that there's conversation to be had here. If there was just some general good cheer directed my way, I could do very well, but maybe everyone was right and I am unfit to go out in public. I cringe when I think about Emily, even though it was so long ago.

Wow, looks like it's time for someone to go home. Fuck you in the end.

All of my memories like salt on a slug.

Sarah and I stay on the enclosed porch with the other people who are too uncomfortable to be inside the party. A small, outside party for the smokers.

After a few more drinks I try to talk to some bored-looking girl about cults, and how the impulses of the cult members might be relatable, if we adjust our perspective. I try to make it an abstract conversation so she can participate.

All she wants to do is list the names of different cults she's heard of. She doesn't agree with what I'm saying and leaves after not too long.

I end up sitting on the ground, alone, with my legs out so that people have to step over me. I can hear Sarah talking to someone else. They seem to be arguing. I can't tell about what. She's explaining some article, but she sounds mad. I can hear her voice going on and on and on.

I close my eyes and say, "Oh blah blah blah blah blah."

I can hear Sarah say, "Just ignore her, she's fine."

Time, I guess, passes.

I don't remember getting home. I don't remember taking my clothes off. When I wake up I don't remember much at all at first. Just that it feels so fucking familiar. I feel completely dry and cracked, my lips standing off my face, rough. Inside of my mouth stuck together, throat swollen, eyes dry, face crunchy, hair crunchy, muscles dry, skin dry, brain dry, and I can't move. I lie in bed awake, unable to move, for an amount of time I can't even really understand. The silence in my apartment is deafening, and my reasons for getting out of bed are absent.

If I hadn't gone out last night, I could have woken up this morning and gone to the museum, the movies, the store, looked at job postings, found a yoga class, called my mother, adopted a cat, looked at my old yearbooks, put on a record, cleaned my apartment.

But what would have been the point, I would be alone no matter what. The volume of last night, the volume of people, the beer, the volume of the sound of my own voice spilling out of me, the feeling of my own voice in my throat, nothing accomplished, the sheer volume of everything I was unable to accomplish last night covering me, a dome, a crate, a cloud, a blanket.

Better to be inside, better to be sick like I am now than to be out not accomplishing what I thought I might accomplish.

Bitter, my whole body, my whole insides, everything about me that my body makes but that isn't of my body—thoughts feelings personality—bitter for having to live in my shitty body, and my body dittoing the sentiment back to its master.

Better to be inside forever.

Each breath is a punishment. I want to stand, walk smoothly to my window, open it wide, feel the chill, feel the winter, feel the wind, and then the sidewalk.

What's inside me struggles for a minute, some kind of tension pushing at the walls of my body, and then it recedes. I lift up, flop back down. My headache comes back quickly, the dry feeling of my body comes back quickly. Good to be sick, good to be alone, good that it's cold, good to stay inside, good that no one needs anything from me. Good to be me, good to be me!

Eventually, I stand and make it to the kitchen. I can't drink water because the water isn't sweet enough. Imagining the taste of the water like imagining a mouthful of mercury. I look for something in the fridge and find a six-month-old bottle of tonic water that Sarah brought over and that I put back, drunk, without the cap on. I take it out of the fridge and drink it. It's cold, it's sweet, it washes my mouth and throat, and it's not until I've finished the bottle that I realize how horrible it tastes, my tongue seizing vomit-like, candy coated.

This is, in some ways, the most normal I ever feel. I'm nude and I'm freezing. I turn up the heat, tiny trash sticking to the bottoms of my feet. I go to the shower, almost crawling, willing myself not to throw up. I get in the shower and feel my body getting wet. I imagine my skin as a sponge. I spend time ripping the tangled knots out of my hair, hands covered in conditioner, knees weak, unwilling to reflect on last night and on the sum of my inadequacies. I wash my body three times and brush my teeth in the shower. I try to floss but I can't open my mouth wide enough. The muscles in my jaw are dry, inflexible.

In the bedroom, I put on a sweat suit I've had since high school, take the sheets off my bed, pick clothes up from the floor, dirty or clean doesn't matter, put them all in the hamper, put clean sheets on the bed, pause to retch and weep, gather all of the pillows and blankets from the rest of my apartment, get my computer, cocoon myself, watch TV. I order a pizza. I drift in and out of consciousness, letting their reality be my reality, eat the pizza, fall asleep with the TV on, wake up with the TV on, in and out, in and out, alone and lonely like I like it.

Doing all of this intentionally, of course.

Intentionally grafting the imaginary lives of imaginary prime-time soap opera characters, hard workers in their jobs at the FBI or in a hospital, working half in the office half in the field, getting it done, wide webs of people, personal and professional overlapping seamlessly.

They never watch TV, they never check their email without event, they always worry about something real, always have a problem that needs to be, and can be, solved. I steep myself in it. They are me, I am them. Their faces crinkle and weep and so does mine.

I remember having dark, hungover days like this when I was living with James. I remember I would sit next to him on the couch, too close, and ask him to tell me everything would be okay. It was something he couldn't or wouldn't do, and I would end up begging him to tell me things would be okay, repeating myself over and over.

"Is everything going to be okay?"

"I just don't know what you mean."

"Yeah, but is it going to be okay?"

"Is *what* going to be okay?"

I don't know, I don't know, I don't know. And I would repeat myself until he'd cave, and for days I'd hear the echo of his mocking cartoonish sympathy ("Everything's fine") and feel him patting me on the head, reluctantly, like I was a crusty dog.

Sometimes, I would walk up to him and squeeze his arm, angry that he wasn't making me feel loved. I would feed him lines. "Tell me you love me." "Why do you like me?" etc. Neither of us liked it. He probably liked it less than I did.

I was embarrassed to be me and needed someone to reassure me that I had good qualities, to reassure me that I was just overreacting or having a bad day.

Or, at least, that's my take on things now.

It wasn't anything like what I see here on the screen, in these shows about jobs, where when someone breaks down enough to ask for sympathy, all the cast gathers 'round— afraid to insult the hero's pride by giving help, but giving it nonetheless.

You can't ask someone to help you without letting them know you're different than advertised, that you've been thinking and feeling strange things this whole time. That you're uglier, weaker, more annoying, more basic, less interesting than promised. Without letting on that your feelings are easily hurt, and that you are boring, just like everyone else. Once you expose yourself as insecure, it's easy to feel resentment if you're not immediately put back at ease. If there's even a flicker, a tiny recognition of your bad qualities, the resentment kicks in, the deal is broken, and suddenly you're both angry strangers, spending hours alone in a room together and completely unsure of why.

But who cares anymore anyway, it's always better to be alone, better this way, better to be able to be yourself with yourself, openly awful. Who cares? Nobody.

chapter 12

The next morning, a Sunday, Monday on the horizon, I soothe myself by cleaning my apartment. All the dust gone, all the trash out and forgotten, all the clothes folded or hidden, ready for company, even if it's just me, even if I'm the only company.

Two days completely inside, swallowed up, the idea of days being wasted laughable, but still the feeling of being pulled navel-first through an atmosphere, each point more frightening because of its similarity to the last point, yet getting harder, grimmer, darker, stiffer, traces of the last bad day, the last bad experience, clinging to me, stuck to me, all my past experiences a collected grime I look through.

Even though my apartment is clean, something isn't right. I still have all of this stupid shit.

I go to my closet, pick a few sweaters, and throw them in

the trash. I turn on *Forensic Files*, look around for some food, and try to feel a sense of accomplishment.

The sky gets dark early, and I welcome the coming days. Welcome the curling of my spine.

Karen has a brief thought about timing, the hot iron and the rolling ball. The fortunes given to the bold. She decides to send a cursory email to the temp agency regarding Millie's performance. Partly to test the waters, and partly to start what might be a longer conversation. She has a few, vague plans.

chapter 13

Back in the office again. I shred the last of the documents and feel completely unaware of what to do next.

Karen approaches my desk, gives me another stack of papers, and says, "Don't let these sit too long, they're sensitive."

"Sure," I say. "I'll do them right now."

I look down, and there are some financials. Karen smiles at me, tight, and leaves quickly. I shred a few of the papers, and out of the corner of my eye, I see my email change.

A bold line appears at the top of the list.

I get the lizard thrill, some part of me that still lives, hoping it's good news, news from home, a kind note, a joke, a message of love, an olive branch, some excitement, some change.

The feeling is brief and mixed with another expectation—junk mail, bills due, newsletter, something from my landlord, the state of my apartment, credit score, debtors prison, scolding, neighbor complaints, someone from my past reminding me that I did something wrong.

I shred a few more papers, hoping to draw out my confusion, my excitement, the possibilities and the mystery, knowing deep inside that it will be something about Thank You Points, shelving units from the Container Store, Mint letting me know I've spent money.

I turn back to my computer and see that the email is from the temp agency, my representative, Julia. The subject line is "update," no question mark, like she has an update for me. I clam up, I almost seize. Should I open it now, or should I excuse myself to open it in the hall on my phone? Should I wait until lunch? Is it weird to open it now, sitting here, to get a live update on what is happening to me right now?

No one is looking, and I open it. I wonder what Karen already knows, what the other women in the office already know, about me and my position. I try to be in the moment, but I'm racking my brain for signs (Karen seemed mad, Karen just gave me more work, I am horrible, I am competent).

The email salutation ends in an exclamation point, cheering me forward to the body of the text. Julia wants an update on my experience. She wants to know if I'm enjoying my time, if it's something I could see myself doing long term, if I've had any feedback from my supervisor, or if there have been any issues. She says I should "be in touch!"

A flood of adrenal toxins enters my bloodstream.

Can I picture myself doing this long term?

My ears start ringing very low, very slightly, and I play out scenarios ranging from a pay raise and a savings account to a fully realized depression that lasts for years and years and finally erases me. I look around. Are they happy? I think about the pay raise again, and my stomach lurches. I stand and leave my desk to go drink water out of the sink in the bathroom, not telling anyone about the email I've just received. Who would I tell? It feels like bad news, like someone I love has just been admitted to the hospital. I shake as I walk down the hallway.

I stand at the bathroom sink, gripping the edges. My ankles give out, and I rub water on my face and wonder why I'm making such a big deal out of this. This is what the plan was. This is what I thought would happen, and this is what I wanted to happen.

In here, in this building, in this routine. Merging, submitting. Moving forward while staying in the same place. Moving forward by staying in the same place.

I could have friends if I had more money. I could be easier to get along with if I had more stability. If I had a real job, it might come with more responsibilities. I guess I've been wanting those. I could be who I wanted to be—calm, cool, self-assured, self-reliant, independent enough to attract people who could enjoy my company because we're all independent people doing what we have to do to get by.

Not like now, not like who I am now, flailing, filled with puke, thinking about death and feeling angry all the time.

If I were a better person, I wouldn't have to be so judgmental all the time. I could be free of it. Gym membership, Instacart. Take Sarah out to dinner to celebrate, join a book club, little steps, money to go out to the movies. I could go to Saturday matinees when everyone else is hungover. I could be one of those people who doesn't drink, but just engages. I have Facebook, I can find out where the shows are, get more involved, be a joiner. Volunteer at the women's shelter again. Apologize to them, they're not mad. Take a trip home to see your mother and *pay for it*. Take her to lunch.

Focus on the benefits of a real job.

I could start meditating. I could stop watching so much TV, just read all the time, that way something else could come inside me and show me what to feel.

My throat tightens, and I realize I haven't been breathing, like sleep apnea but during the day. I can't take deep breaths, and I wonder if the shallow ones even go down deep enough to make a difference. Maybe I should follow my body's instincts and not breathe for a second. It's supposed to be natural, the flow of the breath. Try to focus on the flow of the breath.

A deep pit opens inside of me, broad, expanding, my brain opening behind my eyes, a sweet sting coming to my face, a sneeze but deeper, warming down to my chest, my stomach, the only way to get myself to breathe again is to let the sob happen, and not try to fight it.

Not like you have any dignity left, anyway.

Not like you're strong, you're not strong, you're fucking weak, sobbing here in the bathroom and feeling sorry for yourself. It's not like you're some kind of pillar in the office, and you don't want them to see you cry.

It's not like "Did you see Millie crying in the bathroom? I'm really worried. I've never seen her like that, she's usually so strong and so reliable. I wonder what happened. I wanted to go up to her and just put my arms around her, but honestly

I was afraid—afraid she wouldn't want me there, afraid to intrude. I mean, if it's something that makes Millie of all people cry, it must be something really heavy. I just don't know if I'm strong enough to help support that kind of grief."

Standing in the fucking bathroom with snot running down your face because someone offered you a job. No no no, because someone *maybe* offered you a job. If Karen comes in here, she's going to take it back, and you're not going to have anything. That's what you wanted all along, isn't it? You know you can't actually just crawl into a hole and die, right? Don't be such a little bitch, at the rate you're going, you'll never be employed, so don't sweat it.

Finally my breath comes back to my body, steady and even, and I feel refreshed.

I pee and blow my nose.

I walk back to my desk completely hollowed out, only now realizing, as I breeze by Karen's desk, that I have been in the bathroom for twenty minutes, peeing and crying.

But I got the job!

I find Sarah on the internet and tell her my predicament—that I feel depressed here, but on the other hand I haven't had a real job in more than a year. She says, "Meh, you should take it if they offer it to you, why not?"

I tell her it's not really what I want to do and that it's draining. She tells me, "It's just a job and you can always quit. You should just take it for the pay raise, like I did."

I tell her I'm not even sure this is what they're getting at with the email. I forward it to her.

She says it seems like something. Maybe they're negotiating an offer, or maybe they have something else lined up for me and they're trying to force my supervisor's hand.

I tell her about Karen coming up to my desk and giving me more stacks of paper to shred, and Sarah thinks this is a good sign.

I tell her I'm a little worried about committing, and she points out that it couldn't get much worse than it is already. "And you'll probably start making 15/hour, which doesn't hurt." I tell her I'd been thinking eighteen. She says, "Sounds good."

It feels good to talk to Sarah about this. She's not exactly being supportive, because she isn't taking my distress seriously, or saying anything cheerful, but in a way it does help me manage the dread.

I write a brief response to my temp rep and send it to Sarah. She tells me I should make it more businesslike, so I remove a few pleasantries, and end up sending a two-sentence email that says everything has been going well but doesn't indicate if I could "see myself doing this long term" or not. Sarah says remaining distant will help with bargaining power.

I feel unsure about where I stand and what I want, so I look up some recipes and make a shopping list. As an exercise, to show myself what it might be like to have more money, I go to the Whole Foods and spend $60 on things that will not last long.

The documents sit unshredded on my desk.

chapter 14

At night, I put almonds into a small Tupperware to take to work as a snack, just to try it out. I make a peanut butter sandwich for dinner.

I have a series of flashes. One of them is opening my email and finding an anonymous message that reads "they're coming." Letters arrive in the mailbox of my mind, informing me of a missed court date, outstanding debts, personal complaints about my appearance, demeanor, odor. My hair and neck are still wet from snow and I'm freezing, but hot in my crotch and in my pits. I'm filthy from the inside-out.

I tell myself that change is possible, could be possible right now. Behavior is changeable. I might not be able to change my thoughts and opinions, not at first anyway, but my behavior, that I can do. If I don't care either way, why not make some changes to my behavior? If I'm dead inside already, why not make a few simple changes? At least my body could feel better.

I hear footsteps coming down the hall, and I place my peanut butter sandwich on the kitchen table, light a cigarette, and wait. No one comes for me, this I know. It's time for a complete reprogramming. Whoever walks in the hallway is either tired or heavy, loud thudding and dragging footsteps coming up level by level, closer to my door. The steps are not for me. I smoke my cigarette defiantly. I live here, this is my apartment, nowhere on the lease does it say that I can't smoke, and if that's a rule, I'm happy to abide by it, but you have to tell me the rules before you scold me for not following them.

A key slides into a lock, and I can hear the shunting slam. I notice that my hand is shaking and that even though I'm smoking, my mouth is filled with peanut butter.

I decide to make a list of things that I should do to help carry the momentum of the potential job offer. On my list: call mom, explain potential offer, wash tights in sink, stretch, three glasses of water, no drinking, think about book you might read.

I gather my tights first, digging into the bottom of the closet, on the floor, and in the underwear drawer, smelling them, all rank and in need of attention.

I fill my bathroom sink with freezing cold water and pour in a capful of Woolite, making sure not to agitate it too much, in accordance with the directions on the back of the bottle. *The rules.* I submerge my tights. My fingers move gently through the water and it feels soothing and invigorating, until I notice that the skin on my hands has become rough and dry and cracked, and my forearms (formerly my favorite body part) have become thick and dry with time. They sway slightly with each movement and are no longer obviously muscular.

My jaw sets, and anxiety rushes through me. I recite some insults, self-directed, and then tell myself this is it. This is all.

I wring out the tights, hang them on the shower rod, and call my mother. As the phone rings, I reflect that certain people, people who don't get out too much, people without many intimate relationships, tend to talk too much when they finally get the opportunity. I'm like this sometimes. Talking naturally is on the top of my list of things to learn to do.

Chat chat chat, chatty old me.

When my mother answers, I immediately become bored and irritated. I try to tell her about the temp gig and how I feel about it. I try to remain positive.

She thinks it's great that I might be getting a job offer, and I can hear a delicacy in her voice that I find very upsetting, like she has to be very careful with me, even though I'm the one who called to bring this all up.

"Yeah, so, I don't know. I feel like the offer is going to come pretty soon, but I'm conflicted about it," I say. "Not that I don't recognize all of the potential benefits."

The meaninglessness of it all washes over me again, another intoxicating wave, the floor opening beneath me. *Isn't this what you wanted?* No. When I was a child my mom used to tell me that life was like a game, and sometimes you had to do things you didn't want to do in order to do the things that you did want to do. I always thought this was strange advice. I only ever had brief and fleeting ideas for things that I wanted to do, but mostly I felt completely overwhelmed by possibilities, and then just went down the list saying no, no, no, not that, not that, until I was playing this idiot's game of racking up things I was doing that I didn't want to do in service of some imaginary thing I might one day stumble upon. I try to push this memory out of my mind, but I can't.

"It's fine," I say. "I can do this."

"Of course you can," she says, but I don't feel it. All I can feel is the thin film of stress stretching over me, tight at the neck, tight where my back hunches. I want to cry. No one can help me. I just want to blot everyone out and be alone.

"It's just, you know. I really hate the idea of this job. Everyone there is so ridiculous, and the work is completely meaningless, and thinking about taking the job is depressing. I mean, thinking about where it might lead is completely depressing."

She's quiet on the other end of the line, and I sigh and say, "Whatever, I think this could be good for me."

"I agree. You should take the job if they offer it to you. It might feel nice for you to be able to support yourself for a while. Your dad and I were just talking about this. Not today, or next week, but pretty soon, we would like to start stepping you off of the . . . ," she continues, saying reasonable things, almost too reasonable, and somehow I get the impression she isn't really hearing what I'm saying, isn't really picking up what I'm putting down, and my vision grays out at the edges, and I start talking. I hear myself say something about pod people and the lie of individual consciousness. I don't grasp the whole of what I've said. She's silent again.

"I'm sorry," I say. "It's been a confusing time for me."

I want her to tell me about her confusing times, to tell me the narrative of how she was in my position once, but that everything worked out for her. I want her to tell me that she ended up happy, but there's just silence at the other end.

I tell her that I'm trying to make the best of the situation, hoping to sound mature. Like a dog giving paw or whatever, I'm desperate for her to tell me I'm doing the right thing. Desperate for her to talk me into taking the job, and to do so with enthusiasm, not skepticism. I can almost hear her looking at her iPad, choosing what she'll watch when I get off the phone.

"I just want to be more in the present," I say. An image of everything I've lost comes to me in a crippling flash: James, my youthful vigor, friendship, flexibility, happiness, an unknotted stomach.

She still doesn't respond, except to say, "That all sounds positive."

"I don't know what I should do," I say.

She tells me to wait it out, and, again, to take the job if it's offered to me.

I'm not sure what I wanted her to say. I feel like it's a tone problem, more than anything. I can't put my finger on it.

She tells me "honey it's late" and that she doesn't have anything to report. I say "okay, cool" and I tell her I'm nervous about the job. She tells me "you'll be fine" and I say "yeah, but what is *you*?" I tell her again about how I think the self is an illusion and completely false and argue for that as a reason why I shouldn't be overthinking this too much (and then I laugh and say "I" ironically, waiting for "her" to respond) and I'm talking so fast and not breathing and I can feel my stomach muscles pushing in as I reach to finish my sentence.

My mom tells me that that's kind of enough for her tonight, and I silently commend her for her honesty.

I hang up the phone and feel sick to my stomach. I sit at my kitchen table and fantasize about deep-cleaning my apartment and buying all new things and getting a car.

I get the cooking sherry that I bought for some stupid fucking reason and pour myself a tall glass and smoke by the window, daring someone, anyone, to say anything.

The more I drink in silence, the less likely it becomes that I will move. I want to throw the glass of cooking sherry against the wall. My hand is wrapped around the glass, but I don't believe in free will, so I can't make myself do it, and I don't believe in the individual, so I recognize that my ("*MYYYYYYYY*") impulse to throw the glass is meaningless and a construct, and mostly I'm just tired and on a vague rage blowout and what's the big deal anyway, I'm fine. I feel suddenly quite light and carefree. I don't need to throw the glass across the room.

Each beat of my heart sends a tightening feeling through my torso. A list of things I could have: peace, stability, a clean winter coat, a Swatch, perfume, a haircut, boots both warm and fashionable, a good body, nonthreatening relationships, a clean kitchen, someone to talk to, really I would take anyone. I breathe. I wish I had drugs, weed or Xanax.

I can feel winter air blowing in from the crack in my kitchen window, and I want to jump out of it. Fly home, little baby! I wish I could make myself laugh, relax, take assessment. I will take assessment. I stand.

I put on an episode of *Forensic Files* and turn on the over-head light. The kitchen will be easy. I gather the dishes from the apartment, plates on the bedroom floor, a glass in the bathroom, bowls on the top of the fridge, pans on the stove, and fill the dish-soap dispenser with water to make it last. I scour the dishes as a young woman living in St. Louis has some misgivings about her neighbor, which she expresses to some of her coworkers two months before she's strangled to death in her apartment. The detectives read her emails and check her search history—laptop forensics. Her coworker, a few years older than I am, is interviewed in a purplish dark room with a fern somewhere in the nondescript back-ground. The sheen on her brow catches the light and reveals deep pores. It could be worse for me, I think. I could have a forehead like that.

I collect the rotten food from my refrigerator, put it in a trash bag, and set the bag in the hallway. I can risk eviction for one night, unlikely the landlord will take a stroll through the common areas to see who's been misbehaving. If one of my silent building mates sends an email or makes a phone call to my landlord reporting me, joke's on them, because my plan is to get up at 7:00 a.m. and take the trash out in my pee-jays and overcoat. If the landlord asks me about it, I'll say it was probably someone else, or some kind of mistake, because I don't *leave* my *trash* in the hallway like a goddamn animal, and if he wants proof, I'll say, *Well, it's early, but because I'm such a good tenant, and I want you to trust me, here, here's a photo of the hallway, no garbage, taken with this morning's newspaper for reference.*

It grows late and I mop, *Forensic Files* on auto-play. I scrub the cabinets, inside and out, and light incense. The kitchen is the heart of the home, no one has touched my body in more than a year, and I have a beautiful living space. Bedroom, I'm coming for you next! I take a minute to stand completely still in my kitchen, looking at what I've done. I feel proud. I am going to start getting my groceries on Instacart, and if I feel guilty about the employees getting underpaid, I can always choose to have a cash tip ready, because, as Gandhi says, you should be the change you want to see in the world.

I open the bedroom window to the negative two-degree atmosphere to flush out the smell of stale smoke and sour BO. My shoulders are raging, aching, and I fold the clothing from my ever-present pile, make the bed, spray lavender-scented room spray everywhere. How does everything get so dirty again so fast? Must be me! A man calls 911 screaming about how his wife is maybe dead, and I can always tell a liar by his voice. Acting is very difficult, I know this from all my failed high school play tryouts. Everyone thinks deep in their hearts (at least when they're young, or have the mind of a young fool) that they can act, simply because they have deep emotions coursing through them all the time (haha, "they" "them" "the individual") not recognizing that it's the absence of those things that creates a good performance, that their emotions (fear, doubt, anxiety, arrogance) will override the performance. Or maybe we all think we would make good actors because we lie, because our lives are lies.

I was right, he did murder his wife. It's too late to vacuum, so I sweep my bedroom's area rug. For humor, I put a piece of tobacco-speckled Trident gum on my pillow, like in a nice hotel. I found it on the floor by my shoe.

Everything is looking good. I pace the apartment, my prison! my home! Stress still has me by the shoulders, but exhaustion is coming up a close second. If I had unlimited energy, I would do laundry. Or if I had quarters.

Maybe I'm an embarrassment, I'm not sure.

The sink sludge in the bathroom is the last to go. I grab the Comet powdered bleach and the organic enzyme-based drain cleaner and jump right on in. My first sweat in ages. The mold on the drain stopper is smooth, thick, and black. The drain is done, but the pink mold on the shower curtain? Well, buddy, you must wait!

Something similar to anticipation and excitement flits across my brain-screen. I imagine Saturday, doing laundry and washing my washable shower curtains. Maybe I'll invite Sarah over for an afternoon hangout. We could eat pastries and listen to music—*on vinyl*. And if she's cold from her trip, I could say, "Take a shower if you want," because my shower will be clean, and I will have clean towels, and I could even offer her a clean, soft sweat suit to wear. It would be like we were children with an invisible parent looming in the background, providing the treats and the hot water and warm towels. Maybe we could even go to the park and play in the snow.

I shut my bedroom window and turn up the heat to compensate. I set an alarm and move my laptop to the floor and get on my freshly swept rug to stretch. I read about nighttime and early-morning stretching in a teenage magazine fifteen-plus years ago, back when my life still had a feeling of structure and purpose. I can reach only to mid-shin. It's 1:45.

This could be my life if I let it. I could make all kinds of plans and really take care of myself. I could apologize to my mom, let her know I've been depressed since I lost my boyfriend and my job and all my fake friends during a time when I probably should have been medicated (but not blaming her or anything), but that I'm trying to work on it. I could go to the fancy flower shop and buy her some of those little soaps in the cute packaging, she likes those. She might like those. Send her little care packages from the city, like a normal daughter. Like I'm some kind of Christian or something who values and respects her elders—not that I don't now. We could have a low-key relationship and really help each other out by making the other feel valued, since I have always had the sinking feeling she never felt fully valued, and I should own my complicity in that, to some degree. I could form a kind of twelve-step process for myself, turn my life into a living rehab center (but I could still drink). A Soteria House, but less gross and sad.

I get into bed, nude, alert, teeth brushed, an outfit laid out for tomorrow, bag packed with the almonds and everything. I put the laptop on my stomach and start an Instacart order. Little Miss Popular! I treat myself. I buy a candle. I buy groceries according to my fantasy of what the new job will feel like, taking advantage of all of the monetary perks. Everything I hesitated to buy at Whole Foods goes in the cart, and then some—roses and beer, safflower oil, dried mangoes, quinoa pasta. I fall asleep to the sounds of *Forensic Files*, hoping the battery will die soon so my sleep will be relatively unimpeded.

My dreams are superficial and related to home improvement. There's a slight feeling of dread to them all.

chapter 15

To say that I woke up feeling rosy and happy would be an understatement. There are so many things I could do, so many people in my life who are just a text away. If drinking with Sarah makes me ill at ease, why don't I text Beth and see if she wants to get coffee? Beth always bored the shit out of me.

I make Folgers and oatmeal and make my bed. The coffee is sour and the oatmeal is bland, and I fantasize about the Instacart order that's coming and all the promise it holds.

I remember how going over to Beth's house and hearing her say, without inflection, "I made some baba ghanoush," used to really fuck with my mental. She's a real two-beer-maximum kind of girl, always talking about some kind of paperwork she had to do, some internship that was going well for her, telling me about some kind of research project, her blank face smiling at me while I grinned and said, "Wow, great baba." Beth is the last holdover from my college friends, the only one (aside from me) who didn't move to New York or LA or back home after graduating. I ditched her for James and his friends, who eventually ditched me for James. I have thought about reconnecting with her, from time to time, even though I never really liked her. But she did know me before, so maybe (with the new job) I could practice performing my old self, the confident asshole, and integrate elements of that (the confidence) into the new path. The new version of myself where I am both meek and confident. Last time we were in touch, it was just me ignoring her texts ten months ago. I bet she'd be free for coffee.

My tights are still wet in the bathroom. My attempt to blow-dry them is unsuccessful. I put on a striped sweater and a skirt and some lipstick and suck in my stomach. It looks okay, even though the sweater is a bit too small and the lipstick makes me look crazed. I empty the crumbs from my coat pockets and realize I'm running late. Panic seizes me for a moment, but I tell myself that there's no need for panic, not anymore. I don't do that anymore. I take the trash out, even though it might make me a few more minutes late. I'm making this decision on purpose. Life isn't just happening to me anymore. I'm in control.

I ride the train, pushed up against bodies and subjected to the heavy smells of shampoo and cologne, and instead of being angry, I think of it this way: clean people are touching me. I lean on a man in front of me, then lean gently on the woman behind me. I press my boot against the boot of a college boy, and then quickly retract it. I ride the escalator, without walking, and think to myself, "It's your fault that you're late, not anyone else's."

I pass a gourmet donut shop on my way to work and think, "Next time, next time I'll buy donuts and leave them on the counter and I won't say anything, just leave them there like a little fairy."

I don't smell so bad this morning, so I approach Karen's desk and I smile and say good morning, meaning it, because it is an okay morning. She looks up and smiles and forces out a "morning." It's all going to be okay.

The emails I send at work are playful and sweet, full of a gentle sense of regret, to my eye anyway. Regret for my behavior, regret for losing touch, but a friendly sense of reassessing the things and people that have value in my life. I think the stretching last night really did some good. I assume both Beth and my mother will write me back.

Karen walks by and asks me how the shredding is coming. I tell her I'm chipping away at it between phone calls. She says, "well, don't let it sit too long," and I say, "of course."

At home, I look at my face in the mirror, which is something I used to love to do but now dislike. I smile, and my skin grows tight. This is the face people want to see. My hair is uncut. The layers hang at my shoulders in a Louis Quatorze ruffle, split ends, ragged curls. I get my brush and get to work. I bathe my body in coconut oil and ignore a text message, compulsively thinking *my phone is dead*. I work the oil into my body, soak my hair in it, rub it on my teeth, my nails, giving myself a pampering kind of touch. I work the oil into my eyebrows. I notice hairs sprouting from my neck and chin and vow to tend to them later, as a part of my new beauty ritual. I put a warm sweat suit on my body and turn up the heat and open the windows. I drink four glasses of water. I make plans. I get my notebook and pen. I plan to make several lists. On my first list, I write out calculations of how much I think I'll make in a year with the new job and make myself a rudimentary budget. I should be making about $35,000 a year, which seems incredibly high. I calculate food, rent, light entertainment, and a few more things. If I'm frugal, I should have a savings account by the end of the year. So, a year from now, I can start looking for other jobs. I can volunteer in the meantime for references, and eventually apply for management or admin or copywriting jobs in a setting more in line with my values and interests (those all TBD), and then change can happen organically from there—and, because of my small savings, I won't have to stress. I can quit no matter what after a year.

Or, if I like the showroom, I can use my savings on some kind of a vacation. Maybe go back to Europe, or rent a cabin in Wisconsin with some friends.

The text was from Beth. She'd love to hang, but she's finishing up a big project at work. What are my plans next week? This makes me feel secure. I write down on my list that I should pick a specific time and activity for us and should reply to her text no later than tomorrow afternoon.

I spend the rest of my week this way, planning for my future.

chapter 16

Friday was a normal day and went as it usually did—with everyone doing half-work, acting as if it were Saturday already and like they were doing the showroom some kind of a favor by even being there. Patty and Amanda spent a good twenty minutes on one of the showroom sofas drinking coffee, almost blatantly in view of Karen's desk, perhaps forgetting that they had unresponded-to emails in their inboxes.

Millie left a little bit early again. Karen saw it and checked her wristwatch to confirm. This was unacceptable. She waited about ten minutes and then walked from her desk in the showroom to the back offices.

The stack of papers sat almost glowing on the edge of Millie's desk, abandoned. Karen felt good about this. It confirmed her suspicions that Millie couldn't be trusted with a simple but important task, and it gave her something concrete to take to Lisa.

It was a hit, an assassination. Not exactly a lie, but a contrived circumstance. The ethics of the situation were gray. If Karen could assert that she'd given Millie the task innocently, it would be less gray.

Karen looked at Millie's desk. It had coffee stains all over it. Karen flashed on Millie drinking coffee with sloppy pig-like gulps. She picked up the papers and returned to her desk. It would be best to contact the temp agency again, to further document her disappointment, before going to Lisa.

In a normal world—in a world where Karen was at a higher pay grade and had a better title—she would contact Millie directly and talk out the issue. But this was not the situation, and part of the agreement with the temp agency was that they would handle their recruits.

Karen composed an email.

Hi Julia,

Did you get any impressions from Millie about her frankly sluggish work rate here at Lisa Hopper? I have just seen something that puts me further ill at ease about including her on our team. I had asked her to shred some sensitive files, and while walking back to the copy room, I noticed that the files were still not shredded. I did them myself, but I am concerned that she would leave this undone on a Friday. I am concerned that she is not responding well to my simple instructions, and there is a trust issue at hand. We will not be able to offer her a full-time position here at the showroom, and we might need to look elsewhere for her replacement. I am not sure what Millie's career goals are at this time, but it seems as if she is not interested in advancing in this field.

On top of this trust issue, I have felt slightly uncomfortable with her presence in the office, which I touched on in my email earlier this week. Her wardrobe and grooming are somewhat lacking. In a workplace that values style, it is important that we project a certain look to our clients. She is also very dour and unfriendly in the break room and takes excessive breaks. Being by the phones is not glamorous or fun, but it is seriously important to our company.

I feel very much as though Millie has not lived up to the promise you made regarding your temp-to-hire candidates. I am hoping we can negotiate some kind of refund for our financial investment in her. I would love to be able to use your services in the future. We will be hosting events and will be staffing, and we frequently need workers to cover maternity and sick leave. I have had nothing but great experiences working with you directly, and would like to continue our relationship, however, Millie is not a fit. If you were able to arrange a good faith reimbursement, it would help with my comfort levels moving forward with your services.

We would like to use Millie's services, with restricted responsibility, for half of the following week, and terminate around Wednesday, depending on your response to my concerns.

Please let me know your thoughts, and please feel free to contact me via cell outside of work hours.

Regards,
Karen

The clock turned to 5:25, and Karen stood to lock the showroom doors and switch the lights into night mode.

chapter 17

F eeling pretty good!
My chest clenches and my stomach bottoms out as if
to say "Are you sure?" But I feel sure. Making some decisions today, no doubt about that! Not thinking about certain
things today, no doubt about that!

I look at my face in the bathroom mirror, sallow and
grayish, my teeth yellowing in the cracks, a kind of low
gum line on the bottom incisors, a kind of chapped, painted
look to the lips, actual countable pores on my forehead, di-
vided by a real wrinkle that starts between my once lush and
still masculine brows and tapers out halfway to my scalp. A
not-too-unattractive face, when seen in my memory or
maybe from afar (though when I see it reflected in windows,
the eyes seem exceptionally beady and the jaw stern). Never
mind. I'm not distracted by these things anymore. I tape a

pillowcase over my mirror using packing tape from a time in my life when I needed it, when I moved and sent packages. There's a chunky white substance in the corner of the pillowcase, laundry detergent. I flash back to middle school, Megan Lambert, tall and beautiful, laughing and turning red, saying that the stain on her cardigan was in fact laundry detergent, not semen, haha, what a joke. I'm like her now. Laughing. Haha.

I take a trash bag into my bedroom and go through my clothes: too small, hole, out of fashion, too bold, too ratty. It fills, and I put it in the hallway outside my apartment and go back to my bedroom with a new bag.

I throw away a pair of brown loafers with holes in the bottoms, almost completely crystallized with sidewalk salt—last year's winter boots. I still have my cross-country shoes from high school, fifteen years old but lightly worn. I hold them and close my eyes, visualizing their value in terms of use and pleasure. They go in the bag.

I toss a pair of stained underwear and think about how I'm going to buy myself an attractive, soft pajama set. That's the kind of stuff I like now. A fourth trash bag of my clothing goes into the hall, to be taken downstairs in the morning when I'm feeling more rested.

I find a box, crack the packing tape in a long strip, and face the living room. I spend none of my time here, but I will, once I stop drinking and smoking and start reading and maybe get a cat.

I find little toys, a woman riding two cherries like water skis that I got inside of a Kinder egg, a small blue plastic diamond, a set of false teeth, a bust of Abraham Lincoln, a dancing cookie with a human face, a small ceramic frog. I wonder why I even have these things, why I'm the one in charge of them. I try to imagine anyone giving a shit about these things, and I can't.

I have a framed *Paradise Lost* poster on my wall (Polish design, from an opera I haven't seen, from an auction site, a good deal, a litho) that I've never particularly cared for. Or I did at the time. It came to me in a tube, and when I unrolled it and said "isn't this cool?" James said "it's okay."

Those were the days when I was trying to make our apartment look nicer. It was a lame attempt to assert some kind of performance of femininity or mental stability. An apology for being angry all the time and a gesture of generosity with my new paychecks from the Art Institute. A sweet gift for him. I bought matching towels, and I framed our posters. I bought new plates at Home Goods, painted the kitchen, bought an area rug. In my fantasy, James liked all this. People used to tell me I had good taste, but when I asked him if he liked the towels, or if he had a preference, he told me he liked our current towels, the stained beige ones with twelve-inch threads hanging off them.

During the remodeling, our interactions began to remind me of aloof, bored jocks and their materialistic wives on reality TV, the whining "Honey what do you think, do you like the pewter or the white gold?" met with a thick, barely verbal "Uuhh," the husband looking down, rubbing his cropped hair nervously from crown to temple, sniffing.

I felt simultaneously maternal and childish—aggressive

and fussing one minute ("I just thought you might want nice new mugs"), and lying in bed crying the next ("Sometimes I feel like I don't even exist").

When I wasn't engaging him in one-sided arguments, I was floating backward and away, wondering what I had done wrong, even though I knew. Knew I'd taken things too far, been too mean and too self-centered, embarrassing, and my attempts to be sweet and caring seemed false, desperate, pathetic. Probably even psychotic. One Saturday, I asked if he wanted to meet his friends at a bar, an attempt to show him that I wasn't full of hatred and contempt for them, and he said we should just stay in and watch Netflix, since I was so interested in being domestic.

That was when the cord snapped, though we stayed on for many months after.

But that's all in the past.

I take down the lithograph and turn it to face the wall. I put everything that isn't a plant or a book into a box and I roll up the rug.

I visualize myself getting coffee with Sarah tomorrow, really bonding and getting to know each other, breaking out of this yearlong pattern of drinking, complaints, and misunderstandings. Maybe we could go out for breakfast, play cards, really listen—or better yet, not have anything to say. We could just exist together.

I text to see if she wants to get breakfast.

"Can't really spend money on restaurants right now but I have some beer I could bring over if you want."

The true opposite of what I'd planned, almost as if she's

willfully unable to see how nice it might be—the silent, guileless pancakes.

"What if we just got some coffee somewhere? We could play cards."

"Don't really like cards and honestly can't spend money on coffee."

I'm angry for a second, feeling that it must be a deep lack of imagination that holds her back from fully understanding how wonderful my proposition is, and that I, if I am really being honest with myself today and every day moving forward, don't really need to be around people with that kind of stubborn lack of imagination, that inflexibility and unwillingness to let me take control. No one ever wants to do what I want to do, and I'm so permissive, so "Oh, okay!" all the time, so "Tell me about your day" all the time, that time after time I end up doing things I don't want to do, acting the therapist, toeing my limit with alcohol even though I'm visualizing tea, pretending to be grateful at my workplace even though it hurts to be there, pushing my limits and biting my tongue until the inevitable happens and I snap and say something mean. But I don't need to feel this way. I want to be happy, and I want to nurture my friendships, and I want to be happy to see Sarah, so that's what I'm going to do. I'm happy!

I think about offering to buy her coffee, but then I feel like that's what she was angling for, and I'm not going to do that (be manipulated) anymore, so I let the text hang.

I am looking at clothing I could buy for myself and thinking about making some kind of salad when Sarah texts "actually p bored rn can I just come over tonight?"

Oh okay!

I try to relax. I'm not drinking before she arrives, despite having several nice IPAs on hand from my recent Instacart order, and I have made a mustard vinaigrette to go on a spinach salad that we might share.

She shows up an hour after her text with four warm beers in her backpack. "What's with the bags outside?" she asks.

"Oh, just doing a little house cleaning," I say.

She raises her eyebrows and nods, stepping over my knickknack box and my rolled-up carpet.

She offers me a beer and asks for a cigarette. I give her one, ask if she wants anything to eat, indicating the salad in a large bowl on the counter. She says, "No, I'm not going to eat that. I'm good." I nod and say "cool" and put it back in the fridge uncovered. We sit in momentary silence. She blows breath out of her mouth, puffing up her cheeks either like a monkey or like someone with deep world-weariness.

"Sooo, how are things with you?" I ask.

She makes an immediate mistake, thinking that, again, I will be interested in hearing a story featuring coworkers and family members I do not know.

I don't even try to listen, I just sit, grunting occasionally, "Oh, yeah, Chris, he sounds awful," trying to stay conscious, drinking quickly, hoping it might unlock some latent interest in the narrative. I try to interject, to change the subject to something broader that I might be able to participate in, but my attempt is reaching ("That's like that one movie").

She veers to a dark topic, a trauma that her college friend, clearly suicidal, suffered years ago.

I want to ask her opinion on the clothing I want to order, but we've never done that before. I think, "I really like Sarah's clothes, that is something I value about her," taking a suggestion from an article I read online about how to get along with people. Focus on their strengths. Sarah pauses to take a drink and says, "Ugh, anyway."

I take my opportunity.

"So, I think I'm going to get some new work clothes—and maybe just some new clothes in general."

"Oh," she says. Uncurious, flat.

"Yeah, I was thinking that if I'm going to be committing to a new job that I'm not really that hot on, I should at least enjoy some of the perks."

"They offered you the job?"

"Not yet, but I thought it would be a good idea to get myself in the right headspace to accept the offer when it comes." This sounds reasonable to me. Almost true.

"I can't really afford clothes right now," she says. "I bought these socks a few months ago, they're really expensive, but I wear them like three times a week."

I look at her socks and tell her she's mentioned them before.

"But whatever," I say. "I'm not rolling in money or anything, but all of my clothes are too tight and have holes and stains." This she knows, so I don't know why she's looking at me like I'm the fucking King of France. "And I want to get a few new things. I don't know, I feel like it might help."

"Sure, why not. If you have the money and you don't have any student debt or bills, why not?"

I stare at her. She says she has to pee. In her absence, I stare at the cabinet, completely bland. When she comes back to the table, she asks me if I broke my bathroom mirror and I say, "Oh, yeah."

We talk for a second, and I see her looking over my shoulder.

"What's that check?" she asks, which is a bit rude, all considered.

"Oh, it's from work. I took it on accident. It was from that shredding project I was telling you about."

She makes a face. "You're taking checks home from work? That seems a little risky."

"No, I was taking something else home." I get the email from the top of the fridge and hand it to her. "I was taking this." She skims it. "It's an email about why someone was fired."

She grunts and puts the paper down. "Why did you take it?"

"I don't know, it seemed kind of funny to me at the time. I guess I wanted to read it."

"I guess I just think that seems pretty risky."

"Yeah, you said that."

"I mean, if you're trying to get on full-time there."

"It's really not a big deal," I say. "I don't think anyone notices what I'm doing there. And I'm already full-time."

I stand and bend, opening the fridge, eyeing the check. I crack a beer in the rare silence that fills the room.

"Can I show you what I'm thinking of getting?" I say. "The clothes?"

I recognize that she can't actually say no, even if that's what she wants. Even if all parts of her are screaming no, she can't actually say no.

She makes a face close enough to a nod and doesn't verbally object, so I get my laptop. I wanted her to say yes. I wanted her to want to help me with this. This should be fun. I would be more than willing to help her cultivate a more professional appearance, if that's what she wanted. Working on a project or a problem is something friends do together, to help them bond.

I show her a plaid smock, thick tights, a cardigan, an oversized turtleneck sweater, a button-up shirt, fake suede gloves. She manages an "Oh that's cute" to the button-up.

"I'm horrible with clothes," I say. "I really need a new coat, too, but I'm at such a loss."

She says the clothes are fine and then tells me that I shouldn't worry about it. She mentions maybe waiting until I get the job offer to buy the clothes, and I say, "But you think I should get these?" She says, "Yeah, they're fine. I mean, if you can afford them."

The night is not going as planned. We drink all of the beers and switch to the cooking sherry. I'm frankly not even sure it's alcoholic, but it tastes alcoholic, especially in my mouth the next morning. She still wants to talk about whatever friend or family member with whatever drug problem, and I lean forward and say, "So you guys were pretty close, so that's why you're taking this so hard?" I put my hand on my chin and furrow my brow. "This is really affecting you on a day-to-day level?"

"Well, I mean, no, we weren't that close, it's just on my mind."

"Is it on your mind because you feel that Chris isn't taking your criticisms of his management style the right way? And you feel some connection there, between your cousin's frustrations and your own?"

"I mean, now that you mention it."

"I think the best thing to do in these situations is to just take things as they come. Take it in stride. You can't control other people—you could adopt that as a mantra."

She launches back into the same old story from the top, and I catch a glint of my laptop on the kitchen counter, calling to me. I should pull the trigger on those dresses. The last thing I remember doing with a clear head is thinking about pulling the trigger.

In the morning, in bed with only my pants on, fragments come back. Sarah talking about how some event came right "before her promotion," how some argument between her and her other friend was when they "both got their promotions," the slug in my gut swirling around, gurgling things about "promotions," whispering to me that I am not going to get a promotion, that my promotion is the one that should be in quotation marks, a little voice whispering to me that it all seems a little risky.

Sarah talking about her fabled student loans again while I pulled the trigger on some new dresses for my new lifestyle.

Some garbage stories about people I don't know, flaccid

pickings at gossip, rote monologue, hollow martyrdom. Little digs. Everyone taking little digs.

A pounding in my head like something wants out. A memory of how I wanted today to feel, that memory transposed on top of what's really happening. Not getting calm pancakes with Sarah but hating her deeply, blindly, a barfy feeling as I'm still trying to make the dream possible, still might finish my cleaning project, still might sign up for that yoga class, still might, still might. I step into the shower and almost faint, an image of taking the day by the throat and bashing its head against the wall floating in my mind.

Some hours pass. I put on a coat and other necessary winter gear and leave my apartment. The sun is shining even though it's incredibly cold. I go to the park across the street where the high school has its gym classes. I walk the concrete path around the park, lined with bare trees, circling a small baseball field, a basketball court, a defunct community garden. As I walk, I feel like the scenery is coming at me, rather than me walking through it. I can barely feel my body moving, trees coming at me, feeling the 3-D space, a gray stumpy tree shifting and gliding past me, movie theater roller coaster, rounding the corner of the path, watching the garages, back porches, dumpsters, wires shift in and out of view. Almost transcendent. Feeling myself finally calming down. Feeling my face relax to the point where I can't even feel my face.

I see a dog in the park. I see kids playing on the playground in their puffy coats, parents or maybe nannies on the benches watching, talking. Everything covered in dirty snow.

I circle the park over and over, thinking about my situation. Assessing my life. Where will I go, and what will I do?

I almost feel like I'm flying, light and easy.

I walk for maybe forty minutes in this circle, until a woman in a polo shirt with a whistle approaches me, smiling.

"How we doing today?" she asks, and I wonder if it's really that easy to get people to engage with you, if relaxing really is the key to socialization.

"I'm well," I say, not wanting to stop, feeling myself almost try to walk past her, but her stepping in the way of my path, me pivoting in a certain way, slowing, reluctant.

"So we're doing okay today?" she asks, again. The tone in her voice has force. I recognize it as malevolent almost immediately. I start to get nervous.

"Yeah, we're doing fine today." Haha.

"Been doing a little bit of drinking today, maybe?" she asks.

"Drinking? Oh, no, for sure not. I'm just clearing my head, going on a walk in the park," I say. Then, like maybe it will make a difference, I point over my shoulder and say, "I live right there."

"Seems like you've been walking around in circles and stumbling a bit for almost the past hour," she says. I notice a family in the playground behind her. The son throws a lackluster snowball, his puffed suit moving unnaturally, his mother watching with tight lips. I know she did this to me. Fuck you, I think. Fuck you.

"Stumbling, I'm not sure," I say. "I had a long, stressful week at work, and I'm just getting some exercise." It sounds completely reasonable to me, as it comes out. The intonation is perfect. If we were on the phone, with this kind of intonation, this kind of diction, I could get her to give me her checking account number. Maybe some health details, depending on context.

But we're not on the phone, and the context here is clear: her, in a white thermal under a baby blue Chicago Park District polo, a whistle and keycard lanyard, and those noisy kinds of jogging pants, fogged breath coming out of her, a tight, unforgiving braid almost at the crown of her head, and me in my brown men's overcoat with the lining hanging out the bottom, sweatpants, and cheap snow boots—though I would think she might respond to the sweats, find some affinity there—and my hair still clearly uncombed and freezing in parts from my shower, even though it's mostly underneath my dollar store stocking cap. If only I still had my glasses. It's amazing what a person can get away with when wearing glasses.

I imagine her getting a walkie-talkie call about me, the creepy stumbling man/woman, and looking down at me from her window in the field house, and deciding that she was going to just nip it, just come down here and take me out, get 'er done, as they say, and then her hustling down the stairs, body in full motion, a little articulation of the elbows, a little pneumatic pump of the arms. Nothing really that my ultra-smooth cadence can do to convince her of my innocence in the matter.

"Well, maybe you want to get your exercise somewhere

else, and you can come back to the park when you're feeling better."

"I'm feeling fine, miss," I say, "but I also don't want to cause any trouble." The feeling of relaxation in my body is so profound as I say this that I almost start laughing. I feel light. I feel that it would not be completely out of the realm of possibility for me to daintily raise my hand and give this park ranger a cupped and not too hard slow-motioned slap across her face.

I find it odd that neither of us is leaving and neither of us is talking, and it makes me smile.

"Oh, yes, right," I say, remembering that I'm the one who is supposed to leave. She works here. I think "Toodle-oo," but don't say it, and I walk off toward Augusta, the opposite direction of my apartment. Possibly she thinks I was lying about living nearby, but this is one of those small things that everyone is always encouraging everyone else not to worry about too much—who cares what she thinks of my apartment. Her mention of alcohol does make me want to stop by the local winery for a bottle of their finest, but maybe I should take a hawt bawth instead, what do you think, Chancellor? Oh, Madame, a hawt bawth would be lovely, but I do on occasion wonder if you'll be lonely tending to your own bawth. Will you not be there with me to draw it, sir? Ah, Madame, I would be if it were now, but so many things can happen between the promenade and m'lady's bawth, that promises cannot be made, and wishes might be left unfulfilled.

A light snow begins to fall, little pieces of it kissing my cheeks, my lips, sweet lover, in my hair, cooling my anxiety sweat, making the wetness of my socks in these boots with the hole a little more festive. I take a deep breath, imagining it filling up my brain, then chest, then stomach, and I let it out through my mouth.

The liquor store isn't open yet. I walk aimlessly a while longer, between that space where it would be a gift from the sweet lord Jesus to run into someone I know and get some spiced hot cider, and it being the worst because I'm not wearing underwear and didn't brush my teeth because I was afraid of the potentially mercurial taste of the water. Aimless, giddy dread fills me. I could swoon. I remember that my new clothes arrive on Tuesday, and I say, "Oh, well that's nice," out loud, to no one. I remember that I forgot to text Beth back, and I smile and decide to not be too hard on myself.

chapter 18

I enter the design showroom, again. The wheel continues, blah blah. I find that I am still slightly hungover, even though I don't remember having any fun. Maybe it's the Mondays and not a hangover. Maybe it's the Edwin McCain and the daylight balanced fluorescents and not the result of all of the decisions I've ever made. I try to feel positive.

Karen approaches my desk.

"Hey, Millie. I'm going to reroute your calls to my desk for the day. Our janitor, well, actually he's not really a janitor, but he helps us keep things clean, is out for the day, and I was hoping you could go around to all of the desks and collect the trash bags and then take them down to the basement. You think that would be okay?"

"Sure," I say.

This is what it will be like, I guess. These extra and fluid responsibilities.

She shows me to a cabinet where the large black bags are kept. I go from desk to desk, awkwardly, asking to take the trash. I get glances, nods, a few kind words (but not many). The bag quickly becomes cumbersome and large, and on one occasion, I brush the large black bag against the shoulder of one of my coworkers while she is on the phone, and she pulls her shoulders up to her chin and leans away from me, eyes wide. I don't bother to apologize in the moment but decide that if I happen to see her in the hall, the restroom, the break room, I will apologize and make light of the incident.

I ride the elevator down to the basement. My bag and I take up the space of three people. I don't mind the task, not at all, not today, because today I am feeling sunny and positive about my future.

The door I thought led to the dumpsters, in fact, does not, so I take a brief walk through the second-floor food court, hoisting my bag of wadded papers, empty Starbucks Doubleshot cans, tissues, and damp napkins aloft like an unruly and punishment-bound child. I am momentarily embarrassed by the spectacle, but it's amazing to me, always, how utterly ignored I am at all times. I feel I should make myself into some kind of a thief or murderer.

Eventually, I find the dumpster and get garbage juice all over myself when I deposit the bag.

Not all the stairs and elevators and escalators go to all the floors. The elevator scheme is disorienting. I get turned around easily, finding it difficult, in general, to concentrate while I'm in this building. It takes me about twenty minutes to find my way back to the showroom. I have a bubbling cry-ing feeling in one of the stairwells, and when I finally find the mezzanine again, I want to stop and shove my face full of pizza, but I resist.

When I reenter the showroom, Karen stands and walks over to me. The phones are very slow today. I'm informed that it's common for Mondays, so why don't I take the rest of the day off. I lamely ask if there's anything else I can do and am told, curtly, no.

"Okay, well, I'll see you tomorrow," I say, a bit tight and high-pitched, smiling like a child.

I walk back to gather my coat, shut off my computer. As I leave, I approach Karen's desk with a small white trash bag.

"Forgot to get yours!" I say.

I dip below her desk, head level with her seated ass, and take the small bag of refuse—a Harry & David pear core, a black plastic knife, a few torn pink sticky notes—and I refit her mesh metal bin with the liner, tying it carefully at the lip, taking my time to do it perfectly. She can't even muster a thank-you or a pleasantry about me enjoying the rest of my day, and I leave, carrying her load with me out onto the icy streets and jamming it into the postal-bin-style mouth of the Bigbelly solar-powered trash compactor beneath the train tracks. I walk home, regretting not getting that slice of pizza, effectively free, if it had been eaten slowly and on the clock.

I have a brief thought about the documents and the shredding, but it passes.

I walk all the way home, a bit under two miles, my pits

oiling with my stride, the blood in my cheeks getting crunchy in the cold air.

I feel agitated and out of my routine when I get home.

I glance at the bathroom mirror, still covered with the pillowcase, and I smile and mime fixing my makeup.

I make tea and turn up the heat, feeling the meaninglessness of my moneymaking. Wondering, because I do not know yet, and am still a happy fool, if this is common practice for permanent employees—an early dismissal as a treat for a low workload. Maybe it is really different on the other side. I pace my apartment and wait for the light to dim outside and for my hated routine to come back and comfort me.

I read an article on the internet called "7 Ways to De-Stress." Yoga and exercise are on the list, and it seems like a fine enough idea. There's a studio fifteen minutes away from my apartment, and I decide to call and enroll in a one-month membership. Eighty dollars for unlimited evening access. I can bring my yoga clothes to work and go to the 5:45 class, then walk home calm and hungry.

The woman on the other end of the line tries to upsell me to an annual pass, but I tell her—fox that I am—that I would rather see if I like it for a month before I upgrade. I'm polite and ask her if the annual membership offer is one time only, for new members, and she says that the deals fluctuate, but—I can assume she does this because of how sweet I am—that if I'm patient, I can find a deal this good around springtime. I tell her that I am interested, potentially, in an annual membership but that I'm not yet certain of my long-term financial and living situations. She understands, completely. She takes my debit card information. The hot-pink and neon-blue set of *Forensic Files*, muted, plays on my laptop during the call. The show cuts to a shot of a deep defensive wound, a real one, on a dead female hand, followed by a shot of a living woman, hard and crusted with stress and age, hairspray, makeup, cigarettes, alcohol, the understanding that the defining moment of her life has come and passed and had nothing to do with her, not really, not directly, nodding and talking in the fake pink room, a blurred-out fern behind her.

It seems to me to be a show mostly about construction and façade. The husbands' 911 calls (which they love to play), men screaming "Oh my wife my wife, she's dead or she's had an accident! She's on the stairs or in the tub!" with lilting voices, somehow insultingly feminine, as if to say "if I scream like a girl, something I would never do, they will think I'm in actual shock." We love to see through façades. It's something we've had longer than conscious thought, the ability to tell, subconsciously, that someone is lying to us, like when James would tell me that he did nothing all day at work, but really he just didn't want to talk to me, didn't want to include me in his life anymore.

It's satisfying to hear a lie in a voice.

And in this show, we see it trickle down to the interlopers, their concern, their overblowing of the event of the death and what it meant to them, they're all lying. Are we actually expected to believe that these interviewees were this close to their coworkers? When we hear them tell us that Jenny was a guiding light in the office, are we expected to really believe that? That it was more than just "Oh right, yeah, Jenny . . ."

It's all rehearsed, in a weird way. People spend so much time dramatizing trivial bullshit that when an actual tragedy happens, I wonder how anyone could possibly act out their grief in a natural way. The tragedies we steel ourselves for never come for years and years, and our negative fantasies wear us down inch by inch, so that when the blow actually comes, there's little of us left to care.

The insincere quality of the interviewed coworkers and neighbors disgusts me. I can almost see the layers of "I told you my life would bear great suffering" overtop "but why is no one paying enough attention to *my* grief?" that led these people to sign up for the paid interviews. It's a great fantasy of most people to be interviewed (at least it seems so to me, based on the way most people conduct their conversations as if each self-involved statement is given at great cost and will be received with great interest), so naturally they oblige, because in a way they've been mentally preparing for some kind of interview since youth.

We're so much in our minds, waiting for something to happen, acting it out, that the body and the outer world almost might as well not exist, for all it concerns us.

Which is another reason I think that a yoga class might be good for me. I thank the woman on the phone, hang up, and unmute the episode. I think I've seen this one before. I'm looking forward to stretching. I remind myself of the way I'm going to think from now on. I'm going to practice gratitude and acceptance. I'm going to put myself out there—out there in my body, in the physical world.

I try to cry and think about the things that I'll be grateful for in the future, once I have my life together a little bit more.

chapter 19

K aren was set for her presentation on letting Millie go.
She had the documents ready.

Millie walked in like a goddamn fucking toad in that ter-
rible duffel coat and her salt-covered boots. Looking at her
evoked a kind of smell.

Karen's stomach was in a permanent clench. She could
hear Lisa's voice in the other room, husky, raspy. The voice
of someone who spent a lot of time at the bar or drunk on a
yacht. Slightly unbecoming. If and when Karen was in a
high enough position to entertain clients, she would not take
them to a bar, rather to Gibsons or the Atwood. She would
wear something slim and she would flirt with the men and
the women, she would quietly reassure, she would not take
on a sorority vibe. She recognized that was one way to gain
a client's trust, but smoking and drinking and shouting—as
she assumed Lisa did—were just not her style.

Karen did breathing exercises to calm herself down. She had emails to send, but she couldn't concentrate until she got this meeting checked off her list. No one obeyed the schedule. The meeting was set for 9:30, and it was 9:45. As if Karen didn't have anything better to do than wait around for Lisa and Holly to finish whatever gab session they were having. Sometimes she felt like she was working in a day care center.

Patty and Amanda in textiles were the worst. When clients came in for textiles meetings, they would sit at their desks playing *Candy Crush* or whatever, looking at their Facebooks, updating their gym memberships, who knew what, and the clients would mill in the lobby by Karen's desk. In those moments, Karen had to make small talk with them, had to attempt to be so charming that the clients didn't notice that they had been kept waiting for twenty-plus minutes.

Karen was not at a high- or low-enough pay grade to use her sex appeal in these situations. She preferred to relate in a sterner, peer-to-peer level. She was not servile. She didn't want to talk about the weather, she did not want to tell these people how "gorgeous" their coats were or talk to them about their vacations. She wanted to direct them to where they needed to be and help them schedule site visits and assist, if she could, in the placement of orders, and then have them out of her hair. But, the way things were currently run, with Lisa's top-down encouragement of lax behavior, this did not happen.

So Karen would shake their hands, assert that she was delighted that they were in her showroom (without stooping to any language or body language that might convey a childlike sense of "delight"), state that they were free to ask her any questions, offer them a beverage, sit them down, and go back to work, acting calm, not drawing attention to her anger, all the while using the internal messenger service to chat with textiles, saying, "Did you get my email last week about the time of your client meeting? X is in the lobby, and I don't want them to wait too long. Please advise." And then, after no response: "I would like to be able to tell X how long they should expect to wait, please advise."

It was nearing 10:00 a.m., thirty minutes after the scheduled time for the meeting. Karen walked to Holly's office and knocked on the doorframe. "Is this a good time?"

"Yeah, come on in," said Holly.

Lisa was checking her phone.

"I want to talk about the possibility of starting up an internship program here again. I know we did it over the summer, and we lost our intern before she could transition into her full position here, but I've been doing research, and I do think it's the best way to find a reception assistant who would be able to integrate into the office seamlessly."

"Karen's been having trouble with the temp," said Holly.

"Oh, well, no surprises there," said Lisa. "What's the issue?"

"Trust, communication, and poor work," said Karen.

Lisa raised her eyebrows and shrugged. "Okay, let's swap her out, that's fine."

"The problem with that," said Karen, feeling slightly frustrated that Lisa didn't seem to note the internship suggestion, "and I take full responsibility for this, is that we can't really get another temp. The agency we hired her through has a two-week trial period, after which, the placement fee is nonrefundable."

They stared at her, wondering why they had to hear about this.

"We've passed the two-week trial period, so we're currently in the red. But I am working on getting the agency to reimburse the fee, and I think with this new internship program, we could easily make up the difference within a month or so if they won't reimburse. Again, I take full responsibility for this, and I'm committed to fixing the error."

Holly checked her phone, and Lisa opened her mouth, as if to speak, and looked at the wall behind Karen's head.

"Wait, I don't get it," said Lisa. "What's her job?"

"She's our reception assistant," said Karen.

"So she's just answering phones?"

Karen's irritation blossomed, and with it came defensive hostility, which could be heard very subtly in her voice.

"Well, initially, I'd hoped to have her doing more than that. But when I've given her simple administrative tasks, she's barely completed them."

"You've talked to her about this?"

"Well, her attitude is severely lacking, so I'm not sure how much good that would do, or how much more clear I can make myself when I assign her a task with a deadline. On top of all of this, she's incredibly slovenly, and I noticed that she'd left some sensitive HR documents out in the open on Friday. I honestly don't think there's any further training we could do with her, but I do take full responsibility for bringing her into the office."

Lisa kind of rolled her eyes, but it was mostly impercep-
tible. "Holly, what do you think about all of this?"

Karen's adrenaline was up and her temples were pounding as she stood there in the corner, needing to eat.

Holly sighed, threw her hands up, and let them fall back
into her lap. "I don't know. I've never really interacted with
the girl, but I've never been crazy about temp agencies.
It's always a fucking rip-off, and you end up with these dis-
gruntled losers. It stings to lose the placement fee, but I'm
all for letting her go. I mean, Karen, if you really think she's
a lost cause."

"I do," said Karen.

"Okay," said Lisa to Holly, then, turning to Karen, "Okay."

"Great. Winter internships will be starting soon, and I
think there's a good chance we could find someone who
would be able to commit to staying through spring semester.
I think having someone here who has a design background
and who might be interested in learning how the organization is run from a managerial standpoint would be a huge
asset. And we'd be able to make up the difference in what
we lost with the temp agency pretty quickly."

Holly and Lisa were not trying to hide their boredom.

"I have some information on all the schools' internship
programs, when they start, and what's required on our end."
Karen handed out some stapled packets, which the women
perused, flipping through the pages so quickly they couldn't
possibly have read any of it. "I'm pretty sure I could have
some interviews set up by the end of the week if that's okay."

"Wait, what?" said Lisa. Holly looked down at her pages,

thinking about something else, a TV show she used to watch and was thinking about picking up again.

"The internship programs," said Karen. "From the local colleges."

"For reception?"

"Well, it would be part of a larger arts administration and management internship," said Karen. "This would free me up to take on special projects."

Lisa looked confused.

"We can look into this," said Holly. "But let's hold off in the meantime."

"Got it," said Karen.

It seemed like maybe the other women were waiting for Karen to leave, but she wasn't leaving. "Anything else?" asked Holly.

"Well, yeah, I did want to talk to you both about an idea I had about possibly holding a cocktail party for existing and prospective clients. Something based on the fund-raiser model, but that would just be a way to get our name out there. I think it would be great to open up the space, invite people in, and try to make this year a really full one here in the Midwest."

Lisa wagged her head side to side like a children's toy and said, "Yeah . . ."

Holly tried not to wince, and the motion transformed unconsciously into a wink. "Why don't we talk about this later. One step at a time."

"My idea isn't fully formed yet, but I wanted to know if you were open to it," said Karen.

"Maybe," said Holly. "Is that it for now?"

"Yes, that's about it. I'll put together some more info on internships. And, to get an idea of a timeline on the temp, I'm rerouting her calls to my desk. If the workload is manageable, I'd like to send her home as soon as possible. I'm happy to come in early to compensate for any lost work time on my end."

"Uh, yeah, okay," said Holly. "This all sounds great, thank you. Whatever you want."

When Karen left, Holly looked at Lisa and smiled and shrugged and the two women laughed.

"Well, that was baffling."

"Ah, you know. She's very . . ."

"Isn't she the receptionist?"

"Well, you know. She's a real go-getter. I know we're not going to have a party here."

"I know you know. Wow. It kind of sounds like she wants to be the intern. Do you think that's what she's angling for?"

And then they laughed at her again.

Back at her desk, eating her yogurt, Karen looked at a calendar. If Millie were let go Wednesday, tomorrow, as planned, it would be roughly ten days without any assistance with the phones. After that, the intern would start and Karen's entire workload would change.

She made some adjustments to Holly's calendar, sent out emails to some of the sales reps, and then fantasized, again, about her idea to start a client newsletter. Something the intern could help her get off the ground, no doubt. Ultimately she'd like to have the logo redesigned, but that would be a bigger battle, so it would have to wait until things were a little smoother and more stable.

She opened an incognito window and read articles on brand consciousness, newsletters, and arts management.

People started filing out, looking down at their phones, walking in pairs and small groups. Millie left alone. A piece of trash fell out of her coat pocket. Once Millie was out of sight down the hall, Karen walked up to the trash and picked it up. It was a receipt for a bagel with cream cheese and a large coffee. Karen threw it in the garbage on her way back to the office area. It was deserted. Karen walked to Millie's desk and saw some sloppy piles of paper, a notebook with chicken scratch notes, and two dirty coffee mugs.

Karen got on the train feeling good about what she'd accomplished that day. Her cool fingers wrapped around the pole on the train.

chapter 20

I t's Wednesday, and I wake feeling oddly rested.

I fell asleep last night around 10:00. I set an alarm for 6:45, so I could go on a run this morning. I didn't sleep well or deeply (I usually sleep very deeply), and I think that's why I was able to wake after snoozing for only thirty minutes.

I put on a sports bra (one I've had since high school, but time has stretched it to fit my new proportions), and an extra large sweatshirt from my elementary school, the Washington Warriors, which I have to wear inside out to hide the crude emblem of my alma mater.

I get down on the floor, feeling very stiff and bloated, to stretch. It's painful but still a real triumphal moment for me, doing it more than once in a period of seven days. I lie back and do a few flaccid crunches. I'm only able to continue by imagining that it will be easier later, after more practice. I make a mental note to bring yoga clothes with me to work.

I put on a stocking cap (to finish off my chic look), put my feet into my "fashion sneakers" (turquoise and probably unfit for actual exercise), put my house keys in my bra, grab my headphones, and leave the apartment.

To say it felt good or to say it felt bad to run would both be untrue statements.

There's a little winter slush and a few slick spots, but otherwise the terrain is passable. Within a block, I have that knifelike feeling in my side that I'm sure is familiar to most out-of-shape runners. I can feel the extra weight on my body bounce under my sweats, and the sweat begins to flow out of my skin. I'm able to think of the bouncing flub on my body as becoming oxygenated by my blood flow, the fat cells heating and immediately shrinking. I imagine that over not too much time, the cells will completely disappear. Maybe explode, whatever they do. I will have a new bod.

I realize I'm running at a fast walking pace, so I try to straighten up and break into a healthy jog. I breathe deeply, and the cold air cuts into my throat. I taste blood. How my throat could be bleeding, I don't know, but I remember this feeling from other cold jogs. I'm not worried.

I see people up and walking toward the train with thermoses in their hands—not paper cups!—and I think about how, soon, I will be just like them.

A young woman in a fitted outfit with a blond ponytail passes me, and I watch her get smaller, then turn onto a neighborhood street. The thought of following her crosses my mind, but my legs take me onward to Damen, three blocks short of my planned destination. I get to Damen and

I feel like I'm about to vomit blood in the gas station parking lot.

I don't have gloves, and my fingers grip the shredded sweatshirt sleeves, which are unintentionally beige and smell like the inside of a cast. My frozen headphone cords keep falling out of my ears.

I thought I would be able to run at least three miles—which I had read was average for a run—but I can only make it about a mile. I walk.

Back at my building, I feel like I might faint, and not in a hyperbolic way.

I see the white trash bag outside my door, and the thought of touching it, ever, disgusts me.

Inside, the heater is on, and the sweat increases. I throw my sweatshirt on the ground. The dust in the air of my home sticks—or so it feels—to my body. I hobble to the kitchen for water, sidestepping the beer bottles and cardboard boxes from the clothing I ordered. I feel mucus dislodge from my mouth and throat with every sip.

The shower is painful. The steam is immediate, and I feel very overheated. I take off my shoes and sweatpants and put them on the floor by the trash can. In the shower, I feel like I need more water to drink.

I remove the damp, flannel pillowcase and look at myself in the mirror. My face is red, and my shoulders are almost yellow, waxy looking. My features seem small and cramped. I do my best to dress well and deodorize myself. I use the hair dryer and put on light makeup. I make coffee and throw away my cigarettes. I have one cup of coffee and then pour the pot down the drain and make myself some tea. I am almost calm. I don't feel particularly sorry for myself, and I feel genuinely grateful for that.

I put a set of my least shameful pajamas in my bag (yoga) and leave for work. I might describe my feelings as serene.

All is relatively the same at work. I pour myself a coffee in the break room, and resolve that if/when I am hired, I will bring bagels and cream cheese, maybe even a cheap toaster. I can feel my posture as I walk from room to room. It's straight. One of the outfits I ordered online—a black pencil skirt and a black watch plaid button-up with clean lines, made of an incredibly thin, professional-looking cotton— arrived, and I am wearing it. My hair is in a loose bun, held up by a faded neon-orange hair tie I bought at a clothing store for teenage girls when I was lunch-drinking at my last temp job. It's heavy and it itches, and the core of the bun is still wet. I idly think about getting a haircut. I feel clean. I stand in the copy room, gather materials for the mailers, and place them in a neat stack, paper-clipping them (small side on top, big side on bottom), wondering if white nail polish would be too much, if I'm too old for it, or if it's any good anyway. My hands graze over the stacks, fingers assessing the smooth printing of the brochures. I collate fifteen packets.

I clean my desk and look at the firm's website, learning the year it was founded, which corporations it designs for, and read a few profiles of the CEO in *Home Beauty* and *Elle Décor*. I forward calls, feeling my voice come out calm and smooth. I use the PA system, with a little nervousness, but not much. I feel good. I have soup in the food court for lunch and buy a pack of gum and a bottle of water. I know I shouldn't buy bottled water, but holding it, having it in my bag, makes me feel good. I walk around the block, then right back in. Men on the elevator talk about their business in loud tones, and instead of feeling like a toad or an infidel, I feel blissfully invisible. I say hello to Karen, and she raises her eyebrows at me in response, then turns back to her computer.

It's 1:00 p.m. Four hours left, but that's okay. I read a few articles online. I must have subconsciously noticed that the pile of shredding and the shredder had been removed from my cubicle, but it doesn't occur to me to make any inquiries. I read my horoscope, take an agency-branded notebook, and use it to set some goals for myself.

I see that I have a voice mail from the temp agency, and I listen to it. Julia tells me to give her a quick call after work, because she has some updates on my position. She gives me her cell number. I'm glad I went on the run, because I'm able to get a handle on my nervous excitement. I listen to the women milling around in the office and pour myself more coffee.

I decide to walk home instead of taking the train, so that I can call my rep. I'm near the river when I make the call, right at the Kinzie Bridge. It's very dark and very cold. Lights from the streetlamps and office windows reflect on the dead, black water. I get Julia's voice mail. I leave a message, very polite. "Hi, Julia, this is Millie. I got your voice mail. I'm just getting off work now. I'll be available by phone and email for the rest of the evening. Thanks so much."

I could barf.

Julia calls back almost immediately and is incredibly apologetic—she'd just been heading in the door, she has a long commute, she had to stop by the store beforehand, she hoped she hadn't kept me waiting too long, did I have a chance to check my voice mail? I stop on the bridge, frozen, staring.

"Yes, I did—but I was still at my desk at the time. You said you had an update on the position?"

"Yes, I do." She's so excited and cheerful.

"Okay, great," I say. I'm not wearing gloves, and I can feel a hangnail crack open in the cold wind coming up from the water.

"So, that was actually going to be your last shift at Lisa Hopper."

"Oh, okay." I say this partly overtop of what she is saying. I say it with friendly alarm.

"Yeah, they had a different direction they were wanting to go with the position, and apparently they won't be needing you to finish out the week. Good news, right! You get a long weekend!"

"Oh, okay," I say again, not sure of what else to say. "I don't need the weekend, so I'm available for work again tomorrow, if you have anything. I'm ready ASAP."

"Oh, yeah, of course. So, what you're going to do is just send an email on over to our office with your availability, like you used to, and someone will reach out to you if we think there's a good fit somewhere, okay?"

I don't remember hanging up, but I probably said thank you or something like that.

I pass the yoga studio. The lighting is warm and inviting, the walls are a dusty rose color, and there are a few large, juvenile paintings of flowers hung near the back. It's not obnoxiously modern, and authentic seeming because of that. I think I see the receptionist I spoke with on the phone. I wonder how she got her job. Does she go to the studio? Is that something I could do? Does she have a partner, roommates?

As I leave the studio behind me, I feel an appropriate amount of defeat.

Three blocks down is the nice liquor store. Mostly wine and craft beer. The jog must have really done me some good. My body feels relaxed as I stand there in the aisle, looking at the refrigerated case of beer. I'm listening to something sad on my headphones. Some love song. I've always related to love song lyrics in a different way, usually some kind of mourning of my relationship with myself, I don't know.

A laughing, robust man in a baseball cap and overcoat comes into the store and asks for something specific. I imagine him going home to make some kind of meat for his fiancée. I remember how I pictured my life here before I left home. I pictured a downtown condo (though I didn't have that word for them yet—condos weren't glamorous in my hometown, just apartments for people who couldn't afford real houses—we lived in one when I was little) with a skyline view. I wanted an island in the kitchen, where a yet-to-be-defined "we" would stand and talk while making food.

I get a six-pack of something mid-priced and put it on my credit card.

Oh, pitiful walk back to the apartment! Oh, pitiful pacing in the apartment! Oh, agitation! I put on music and drink and pace, not wanting to return to my nightly routine of watching television. It occurs to me to just show up again tomorrow. That fantasy-raise had called to me, and I had answered. Stupid me. I claw my arms and force myself to cry, and then write what feels like a professional and friendly email to my handlers at the temp agency. I express my thanks for the opportunity at the design firm, my regret that it did not work out, and my interest in continuing work as soon as possible, in any capacity. I keep it brief, I think. There's no one else to talk to.

I feel awful. I know that drinking causes a kind of chemical depression in me, especially when I do it alone. I get into bed with the lights on and squeeze my pillow in my arms, longing for someone to talk to, or longing for no one to ever look at me or talk to me ever again. Either one. I don't care.

Naturally, I feel a little better in the morning, for the first few minutes. The adrenaline starts kicking in again when I approach the coffee pot around quarter to noon, just to stare at it. I want to be linear again, like I was yesterday. I know I have to check my email. I know I will have to get another job.

chapter 21

It's not exactly a liberation, getting what you secretly wanted. This is my sage takeaway from being fired.

The coffee starts to brew, and I find my phone and plug it in next to my computer. I don't brush my teeth. Sarah texts me just to say "ugh" and then later "fuck this sexist bullshit, I'm out." I set my phone face down and silence it.

I open my email and then quickly open another tab so that I can't see what emails I've gotten, but I see the telltale (1). Clicking back, I read:

> I am out of the office. If you need an
> immediate response, please email Amanda
> at amanda@officejobs.com.
>
> Julia Connolly

I pour myself some coffee and write:

Hi Amanda,

I reached out to Julia via email yesterday regarding my availability, and I received an out of office reply. I'm available the rest of today, tomorrow, and all of next week. I also have weekend availability, if something short term comes up that you think might be a good fit. Thanks for your help! I hope this finds you well.

Best,
Millie

I immediately receive:

Hello, I am away from the office with limited access to email. Please contact Diane at diane@officejobs.com in the interim. If you require immediate assistance, please call the main office line, and our office manager, Stephen, will do his best to assist you.

Amanda Manard

The sky is bright. I drink two cups of coffee, light a cigarette, and write:

Hi Diane,

I just sent my availability to Julia and Amanda, but they are both currently out of the office. Amanda's out of office reply suggested I contact you. It's nice to make your acquaintance! I am free tomorrow, and all of next week, and am open to weekends and both short and long term placements. I've primarily worked with Julia in the past, but please let me know if you have any assignments that might be a good fit. Let me know if you'd like me to send along my resume, or if you have any questions.

I hope this finds you well,
Millie

I'm unsure of where the line is between seeming responsible and seeming pushy, but after three hours pass, and I hear nothing from Diane, I call the office.

"Hello, Chicago Office Jobs, this is Stephen, how may I help you?"

"Hi, I emailed Julia and Amanda about my work availability, and I got an auto-reply that said to call the main line. Can you help me with this?"

"Umm, sure, yeah . . . hold on . . . what was your name again?"

I tell him.

"Okay, great. I'll pass along a message that you called, and someone will get back to you."

Weeks pass.

chapter 22

I look online for reasons why this might have happened to me—why won't my temp agency return my calls, what to do when your temp agency won't call you back, signs you blew it at a temp job, signs you are a bad employee. I feel myself drowning in days, money running out, parents vaguely aware of a situation that I have spun as positively as I can, an intern possibly taking my position for free, the company deciding that my position was redundant. We talk about the economy, my parents lightly urging me to take this time to think about my future as they transfer me money for rent and food. I promise to work on my résumé and apply for one job a day, and to consider volunteering in the meantime to account for the gap in my employment.

I suggest that I might be able to take a class, and my mother's voice stiffens as she says I should take this one step at a time. She must remember all the classes I've taken,

Illustrator, bartending, grant-writing, ceramics, back in the days when I had enthusiasm but no follow-through. I'm sure she can hear it in my voice that now I have neither.

The texts flow in from Sarah, wondering where I am and if I want to get a drink. I beg off and say I'm busy, have a cold, I'm too tired, and other times, in an attempt to set a precedent, I mute my phone or let it stay dead for days on end.

I finish, somehow, incomprehensibly, the entire fifteen seasons of *Forensic Files*, smoking in my coat by my open kitchen window, bracing myself each time footsteps fall in the hallway for the knock, the final nail, complaints, my landlord wanting to take a look around to make sure everything's okay. The cops.

I take a look around. Dishes on the counter, dirty dishes even in the drying rack, an empty box of cereal, eaten dry, on its side on my kitchen table next to a full ashtray, ashes on the floor, piles of old mail and receipts in the living room, socks, rings of salt on the floor, books and extension cords and Christmas lights covering one half of the couch, dying plants, underwear everywhere. My bedsheets, which used to be white, have a grayish tinge in the middle. Bowls on the nightstand, coffee mugs on the floor.

There's an acrid smoky smell like pee and cigarette butts. It's a smell from childhood. My neighbor's house. "The twins," who were two years younger than I was and didn't look alike. One of them was chubby and brunette, the other one was skinny and blond. The blonde was accused of hitting a sick kid (some kind of bone marrow thing) on the head with a plastic truck. Their mom never seemed to be around, and we had free rein of their house. Sometimes, I would look outside my kitchen window, and they'd be sitting on my fence looking at me, like cats or squirrels, posing, sexy already at six, pure Sally Mann. They were cooler than my other friends, but meaner, too. We said fuck together, climbed the evergreen, ate marshmallow fluff from a jar in their bedroom. When I loaned the blonde my favorite off-the-shoulder pink cotton sweater, it came back reeking of their house, and I made my mom soak it over and over to get the stench out, angry at them for smelling bad, angry at them for being so rough, punching me in the arm, always threatening to push me out of the tree. I brought my new Etch A Sketch to their house, and the blonde stepped on it. I sat on her chest and grabbed her throat, twisted her arms until she wept, the animal inside of me released. I wanted to kill her for ruining my sweater and breaking my Etch A Sketch three days after Christmas. Her mother ripped me off her and screamed at me to get the fuck out of her house. "Get the fuck out of my house!" The hurtful talk I had with my parents, the humiliation of what I had done, but more of what I had felt, all that rage, the mark of her thin heel on my Etch A Sketch for years after, what a stupid toy, wishing I had just let it go, not cared, not even spent time with them in the first place, my bedroom now smelling like all those feelings, all that rage still alive in me, useless and embarrassing.

For food, I am down to licking peanut butter out of three nearly empty jars. I don't brush my teeth. I wake at noon and leave my apartment only for alcohol, which I drink while I search the internet for reasons why I might not be happy.

From a certain angle, the way I've decorated my apartment—scraps, rolled carpets, boxes, exposed food—is nest-like. Some days I walk through my creation, surveying it, detached, almost proud. Other days, I lie in bed under the covers unable to move, unable to even cry, feeling a hatred for myself so wide and endless it's almost funny.

chapter 23

Downstairs from Millie's apartment, Kim and John were on the couch talking about their days. John had spent the day at work and was having some minor conflict with a coworker, which was transforming into a drama that shaped not only his days but the entire narrative of his life. This coworker was lazy and was making John look bad, or that's how he felt, and he was unsure of whether he should confront the coworker or learn to manage his expectations. John went to bed thinking about this conflict, and there were five minutes every morning where he did not think about the conflict, but then it sprang again to his mind, defining his day. He sat on the couch describing his utopian ideas of how the workplace should function to Kim. He imagined the coworker changing her behavior, and he described the imagined change to Kim, who was struggling to concentrate on his words, struggling to find an appropriate response, but the words that sprang to her mind (the ingredients of the dinner she had prepared, an article she had read, whether they should visit her family in the coming months) were completely unrelated.

She forced herself not to say the words aloud, remembering with sharp disdain the way her mother, when she was a kid, would veer off topic during Kim's confessional speeches ("Amy keeps buying the same sweaters as me and then pretending she's not copying me." "Oh look, a new Starbucks!").

Kim and John had discussed him not bringing his work home so much. They had talked about how life was more than just the office. They made plans to read before bed, the same books, perhaps out loud to each other the way they did in the early years, so that when they talked, it would be on a topic they both could enjoy.

Kim said, "Everything will be fine."

"I know, I'm sorry for ranting," said John.

"I'm going to make some tea, do you want some?" asked Kim.

John made a confused and frustrated noise and then, with a snippiness that Kim found womanish, said yes.

They would likely watch television next, with the suppressed and awkward idea that they could have a discourse about it afterward.

In the kitchen, as she often did, Kim smelled the phantom stink—an odd mixture of rich, beefy shit, cat urine, mold, and garbage, with a hint of an ashtray smell—familiar from her days at Michigan State, living in the pseudo-freegan co-op where, one week, they ate recalled guacamole-flavored Doritos from the dumpster behind the student union. She was nineteen then, a sophomore, the youngest in her class, and open to experimental ways of living, which she liked to think helped her now. She'd gotten it out of her system, knew what it was about, and no longer needed it—the "it" being vulgar and desperate ways of living justified by the false pretense of nonconformity as a sign of intelligence and authenticity.

She put the kettle on (enamel, burnt orange, Crate & Barrel, a gift) and got two mugs and the box of ginger turmeric tea (to temper the nightshade from their dinner—a tomato, chickpea, and bell pepper curry) and thought that it was her turn, perhaps even her right or duty, to mention the stink again.

"Will you come smell this?" Kim asked John.

John came into the kitchen, and they walked around the sink, the refrigerator, the bathroom, the garbage, and back again.

"I've tried Drāno, I've scrubbed the trash can, I've cleaned the oven, there's baking soda in the fridge, there's no reason for this smell. It's certainly not the food we cook. But you smell it, right?"

"I prefer not to think about it."

"Do you think it's our upstairs neighbor?"

"I guess that's possible," said John. "But it's probably just the pipes."

Kim looked at him, shook her head.

"The smell happens at these intervals, it's usually in the evening and on weekends, and I can hear her walking around up there. She's been hammering and pacing a lot lately, and the smell always goes away during the summer and comes back when the weather gets colder, when the windows would be shut. It's such a festering stink!"

"Should we ask her about it?" asked John. "We could ask her if she's smelled anything. Maybe we could get a look at her apartment, too."

"I'm thinking of just asking the landlord if he's had complaints about a smell, and then maybe he can ask around. If my landlord asked me if I'd been smelling anything odd in my apartment, I would probably make some changes."

Kim brought up the weird wailing sounds they'd heard last weekend, and they laughed about the possibility of a haunting, until Kim brought up the more likely possibility that their upstairs neighbor was a freak having a breakdown.

The letter to the landlord would probably be the best COA, but they would have to do some recon first.

Kim took off her earrings (they were noisy), and John put his carabiner on the vintage kitchen table they kept in their dining room—a table covered in books about organization, spirituality, culture, art. Kim felt her body tighten, as if this is what she had been training for, the squats, the treadmill, smooth limbs in high-waisted dark gray corduroys, quivering breast beneath a reddish-brown cropped mohair sweater. John asked if he should take off his Pendleton jacket-shirt, and Kim whispered, "Leave it."

They went upstairs on tiptoe in their thick, clean socks. Kim's hand touched John's shoulder on the landing as if to say "should we turn back?" John shook his head no and took a few exaggerated, mincing steps.

They walked to Millie's door, careful not to get caught.

They saw a large white bag of garbage by the door and heard the muted voices and music of laptop television from within. John pressed his ear to Millie's door and nodded. Yes, she was home. They would have to be careful. Kim bit her lip. She wanted to giggle. John buried his nose in the crack by the doorknob and breathed in noiselessly while Kim bent to sniff the outer wall of Millie's apartment. John made a wafting gesture with his hand and moved his head back and forth, assessing, a sommelier.

They heard a crash and human muttering. John made a quick gesture with his hands, like they were in Vietnam from a movie, fingers pointing at his eyes, flapping side to side and then pointing to the hallway leading to the back steps. Kim giggled and turned, scampering. Her socked feet made soft thuds, her corduroys croaked, and John followed her, slipping a bit and almost falling on the stairs.

The decision was made to send an email to the landlord, easy wording, no accusations, that there was an odd smell in their unit, and maybe he had heard other complaints? Which would prompt him, if past experiences could be used as judge (email from last winter asking if they had seen any cockroaches—certainly not), to send out a group email, which would start the process.

Kim and John sat on the sofa and analyzed all of their neighbors for a minute, not just Millie, she wasn't special. They shifted their insight to a friend of theirs—a lesbian—who they thought was a womanizer. They shared secret words about the double standards of that, the political ideas behind that, saying things they couldn't say to other people, but that they loved to say to each other. Kim thought, *Now, this is the man I fell in love with*, and ran her fingers, idly, up and down his thigh.

The next morning, a sense of play was in the air. It was one of those things that was arrived at gently, at an angle, which seemed appropriate to Kim as she reflected on the whole nature of *play*. Relaxation, experimentation, curiosity—a loosening of the pressures of routine life.

She wore her silk robe, which was normally decorative, hanging in the bathroom.

Kim stretched and thought about how she might embody her natural, playful tendencies more. She looked at the philodendron and thought about how plant care was a satisfaction but not necessarily a playful act.

John woke and said "Good morning" with a sleepy, scratchy note of happiness in his voice. The bathroom door shut, and she thought, "That's my man," as she listened to the loud stream of urine.

She opened the laptop and started a new email.

When John sat down at the kitchen table (the one directly beneath Millie's), Kim handed him a bowl of yogurt and raspberries and poured him a cup of coffee. She moved a lock of hair from his forehead and said, "Should we write that email?"

John looked down to where her robe was opening in the front, shifted in his seat, and said, "Yeah, sure," but he said it kindly, not dismissively. "Thanks for making the coffee."

"Happy to do it," said Kim. "I want you to have a good

day. There's no reason why you shouldn't. I think we're both a little hard on ourselves."

John nodded, still slightly lobotomized from sleep.

"Okay," said Kim. She started typing, reciting the words as she went. "Hel-lo Mar-co comma."

After John left, Kim washed the breakfast bowls and thought again about a new approach. Waking early to make coffee and breakfast, like plant care, fell in the category of satisfaction rather than full experimental play—though she did think that any change in routine might help bring out that mental flexibility she was looking for. Kim remembered that she had that Gestalt therapy book and made a note to open it up again. No harm in using a resource.

Marco got these kinds of emails once or twice a year. Is there a smell in the apartment? "Yes, of course there's a smell in the apartment," he thought. "It's a 120-year-old building, what do these kids expect?" It was the pipes. Possibly, but very unlikely, something dead in the walls. He sent a group email to the tenants, as he always did, just to appease.

chapter 24

In a masochistic moment, I email Julia again, asking if there is any possibility for work in the future through the agency. This was advice from the internet. I also ask if there was any feedback she could give me, any improvements that could be made. Like a madman, drunk, in sweatpants, bedraggled locks, I focus my energy and craft a polite and unassuming missive. The response is as follows:

Millie,

You were one of our top workers, and we promised Lisa Hopper that you were prompt, friendly, and neat, with an ability to adapt to a variety of tasks, and with very impressive work history and education. They were disappointed with your performance, I'm sad to say. It was not the right fit for Lisa Hopper. They expressed concerns about your enthusiasm for the job, and also your trustworthiness. Apparently, there were sensitive documents that you were asked to shred, which you left on your desk for days. This put them in an awkward position and also put us in a difficult position as well. We had hoped to place you there permanently, but due to concerns over your performance, your role at Lisa Hopper was cut short. There were also concerns about your appearance and attitude. We were shocked and disappointed to hear you described as unkempt and unfriendly.

We take relations with our clients very seriously and are unable to place you at this time. My advice to you would be to gain other work experience, and, if you are able to present us with references that can speak to developments and progress as an administrator, we might be able to meet with you to discuss reinstatement.

Again, we take client concerns very seriously, and we rely on our workers to represent us when we send them on assignment. I hope you understand.

Best,
Julia

I respond:

Hi Julia,

I'm sorry to hear that I didn't represent the agency well during my time at Lisa Hopper. That was not my intention, and I believe there was a miscommunication between Karen and me. I should have checked in with her more regularly. When I was given the documents to shred, I was told that there was no hard deadline for completing the task, and that it should be done during down time. If I had known that that task was to be prioritized, I absolutely would have completed it more quickly. I was balancing the shredding with answering phones and assembling mailers for new clients.

In response to the criticisms of my appearance, I'm not quite sure what to say. I can assure you I've never gotten this complaint before, and if a note on dress code had been presented to me, I would have happily accommodated. I can't think of an outfit that I wore that was inappropriate, but I understand that nuance—particularly in a design setting—is important. I'm certain I was friendly with the staff at Lisa Hopper but was reserved in my role there, as I observed how busy the employees were, and was trying to respect their space.

I hope you will reconsider, as I've had great experiences working with you.

Please let me know if there's anything I can do, or if you have time to talk about this on the phone.

I hope this finds you well,
Millie

The shit eating is meaningless to me.

I sit at my kitchen table, completely curled, my stomach completely like some kind of garbage awful fist. I get an email from my landlord, asking me if I've noticed a smell in my unit. I do something I haven't done in a long time. I reel my arm back and slap myself full force in the face three times. Kind of stupid to do it completely alone here like this, no one to see what the fuck I'm doing, but whatever.

My mom calls and asks if I want to come visit home for a while. She thinks, and I'm inclined to agree (either that or I'm feeling passive), that it might help me. She will buy the Amtrak tickets.

I don't pack a bag.

chapter 25

I enter the station through a side door and walk along a beige stone hallway, tracks to my left, waiting room to my right. The tracks announce themselves "track number 22" "track number 16" "track number 25" in an overwhelming cacophony. I assume it's to help the blind find where they're going, to help them not walk out onto the tracks, but I can't imagine it being helpful.

There are the usual Amish people and tourists heading back down south toward St. Louis, for some reason forming a line, standing for hours, I assume to get a good seat—or maybe because they think they need to stand, think they're doing the correct thing, but you can just as easily sit before boarding, which I do.

Most of the riders have shopping bags, as if they can't get all this shit online. The grand homogeny. Some have oil-soaked bags from Garrett's. A happy memory threatens to surface. I let it pass.

We all board after passing the overweight, depressed-looking Charon in the hallway, who continuously shouts, "Have your IDs ready!" She screams it at me, while holding my cracked phone and checking my e-ticket.

We exit through Chinatown, through the shabby areas, into the grim non-suburbs and then into fields. We pass Joliet, where the prison is. More fields. A few small towns I think about exiting in, Dwight, for example. Or maybe I'll never get off the train, just ride it back and forth forever.

I get off at my stop, Bloomington-Normal, and find my mother standing by the Subway sandwich shop.

"Hey," I say.

She smiles the kind of smile where your lips disappear and your eyes look worried. Disappointed. She pats my back. We drive home in silence. The light seems nicer here, and I wonder if I'll ask them if I can stay, wonder if I can tell them some story about why things have been so slow or difficult for me, some story that will get my mother to take care of me, fix me up, set me back on track. I could tell her that things have been difficult and lonely for me, and that I think I need to start taking some kind of medication, even though I hate medication and doubt it really works.

It could be like when I had a paper due in school, and my mom would take me into her office and let me lie on the couch with a box of Kleenex (for my tears) and a bag of chips (for my nerves) and dictate my ideas on *Macbeth*, *Catcher in the Rye*, *Huck Finn* to her. Those times were terrifying, but

I look back on them fondly. Quality time. I was always furious when my teachers accused me of plagiarism.

When we get home, my dad is in the kitchen making pasta by hand and listening to something contemporary and god-awful on Pandora.

The dog, my replacement, a taut, bitchy terrier named Cindy, approaches me, barking nervously, tail between her legs. I ignore her. This is the only instance in my entire life where someone's shitty behavior toward me is actually rooted in jealousy. I feel almost complimented.

My mom goes to the cabinet, gets out a bag of chocolate-covered pretzels, and places them ceremoniously in my hands.

"Here. Your therapy."

I scoff, but I could cry. I place the bag on the counter.

My mother sits on the stool at the kitchen island and opens a glass jar of home-roasted almonds, while my father, at the hand crank, explains how much cheaper it is to roast your own almonds. They've both just retired, and this is how they are now. I eat a few almonds.

Light comes in at a slanted angle from the window above the sink, and my parents laugh and tell me about the ongoing construction job that their dipshit neighbors are doing. The house is currently unoccupied, and my mother's main concern is raccoons. My dad says something about odd work hours and debris. My mother walks over to the window with her hands in her pockets, gets on her tiptoes, and says, "Look, look at that—they just have fucking plastic tarps in the windows."

I join her, and while we're looking at the blue plastic tarp making it billow, in out in out, like the breath of the house, my mother puts her arm around my waist and gives me a squeeze, and I say, "Yeah, that sucks," pulling away slightly.

My dad starts to giggle and tells me about a time in September, when the weather was still beautiful, he was having a glass of red wine under the pergola in the yard when a fly (coming from the other neighbors' dogshit) landed in his glass, and he threw the glass of wine over his shoulder and it got all over the side of the neighbor's white garage, leaving a large, gruesome stain.

My voice comes out, "Must have been a big glass," monotone and unbidden, relaxed and remote.

My dad laughs again, a wet, forced sound like the beginning of saying "shit."

My mom laughs and says, "Oh yeah, he was . . ." and then makes the universal hang-ten wobbling motion to indicate heavy drinking. He catches her from the side of his eye, as he was meant to, and says with practiced disdain, "Yeah, I was," eyebrow raise, slight pause, "*wasted*."

"Well!" says my mother.

A timer goes off. Pandora offers to give us thirty whole minutes of free music if we watch a short, wordless video.

"You have to tell her the second part!" says my mom.

"What are we drinking with dinner?" my dad asks.

"We have plenty of booze," says my mother, throwing open the refrigerator with bravado, for my benefit. I see rows of Sam Adams and Coors Light, four bottles of white wine, and I hear that there's hard liquor "by the dog food."

"Your mother had her book club over and bought two thirty racks."

"They were not thirty racks."

"I don't know what she though the geriatrics were going to do with it all."

"Well, you never know what someone is going to want." The defensiveness in her voice is so playful, the hurt so mock.

"Your mother's a great host."

"But tell her what you did," says my mother.

The neighbors have their "property" (the word spoken with that disdain again) gated, so that no one can break in and steal their construction tools, so my dad had to hop the waist-high chain-link fence with a wet rag to clean the wine off of their white garage. I imagine my dad's ass in the air as he does this, and I smile, imagining my mother standing guard for the B and E, nervous, maybe holding a flashlight, whispering "David, hurry."

They laugh again while telling me this. My dad asks me if I want to put the pasta in. I shrug and walk over.

I pick up the scraps of dough and lower them into the pot of boiling water, while my dad tells me about Spoetzl, and how they just throw wads of dough into the pot and it comes out looking like a sea sponge.

I don't want the sun to dip any lower.

My mom tells me that these noodles are so fresh and delicious that they taste almost creamy. One time, they used a cream sauce, and it was inedible. One of them makes a joke about how they ate it anyway.

"Plates or big-boy bowls?" my mother asks. My father rolls his eyes, shakes his head, and sighs.

"What? That's what we call them!"

We eat from the wide, shallow bowls from World

Market, on the couch, watching the news. They were right, the pasta is creamy. My mother says something about how she "can't watch this" when a particular figure comes on the screen. I'm honestly not even watching. The dog is seizing with anticipatory delight on the rug by the coffee table.

The television is in the center of a wall of built-in book-shelves, floor to ceiling. The dining room also has built-in floor-to-ceiling bookshelves. Space on the walls not taken by books is obscured by large, tropical-looking plants, fig trees. A low shelf under the window has four large geranium plants in full bloom. Paintings from the university's fire sales on the walls. A drawing done in wax.

I notice something I haven't seen before, a three- or maybe four-foot puppet of my dad, hanging from the side of the bookshelf. My mother has captured him so perfectly, the khakis a few inches too short, the re-created Merrell slip-ons, glasses, a buzz cut. It's a sight, my father hanging there in miniature, that could be macabre but is endlessly com-forting. I'm hit with layers and waves of indiscernible feel-ings. I say, "Cool puppet," and my mom says, "Oh, yes, I'm making one of me, too, for the other side."

"Cool," I say again. Then, "I like it."

"I can show you," she says. "Your father probably isn't long for this world anyway," she says, meaning sleep, but we both say "Jesus" and laugh.

Upstairs in my old bedroom, my mom shows me the proj-ects she's been doing since retirement: a shadow box, some collages. "I can't draw, obviously," she says. On the desk is a pile of fabric that will become her once she gets around to it.

I say that it's all very cool, and then tell her I'm pretty

tired. She gives me a hug and says it's good to see me. The hug lasts a minute too long, and I feel a sting in my chest.

Night falls, and I can hear her on the couch downstairs watching TV, the dog's collar rattling. I'm watching *South Park*. I wonder if she ever cries for me, or if they're worried about me, and then cry myself to sleep.

In the morning, she takes me out for coffee and bagels, plural. I eat two, one with tomato and sprouts, and the other with honey walnut cream cheese, which my mother forgivingly says is my dessert. I tell her I'm freaked out. She tells me she's not worried about me, but that my clothes are a wreck. We go to the mall, and in the parking lot she says something to embarrass me like "let mama take care of her baby." I snort and say "Okay, Mom."

She replaces my coat first, then buys me one professional outfit, and a pair of Clarks desert boots. We go to the GAP and she buys me new jeans, two new sweaters, and a hat and gloves. We go to the department store and she buys me age-defying night cream and lipstick. She tells me she knows it's no big city salon, but she could take me to Marissa at the Paul Mitchell school if I want a trim. I let her. Afterward, we go to the Target, and she buys me pajamas and new underwear. I'm new. I change into new clothes and underwear in the Target bathroom, and my mother nods at me as I emerge and says, "This is also for my sanity." I get what she's getting at.

We meet my dad at Lucca Grill and have pizza and salad and a lot of beer. My dad tells us we both look very pretty, and it's simple, but it feels very nice. We talk about politics. My mom talks about Louise Bourgeois, and my dad talks about Alan Watts, and I listen, but I also have things to say, and the opportunity to say them. When I move my head, I can feel the hairs shift all the way up to my scalp.

"Do you remember when they used to have a violinist here?" I ask. "I think I asked him to play 'In the Hall of the Mountain King,' but he didn't know it, so he played, like, some children's song. I think I was openly offended."

"I don't remember that, but I do remember you on that 'Getting to Know You' board in Ms. Schmidt's class."

They both laugh.

"Those little Polaroids of you and your classmates. They all listed *The Lion King*, Jesus, colors, family under their favorite things, and you said your favorite film was the PBS version of Wagner's Ring Cycle, and your hobbies were foreign films and painting. God, they didn't know what to do with you."

"I wanted to be a dentist."

"Well, I never knew about that."

"Do you remember when I quit the basketball team because the coach disrespected me?"

"Yes! It was one of my proudest moments as a mother."

"I remember you body checking those girls at the games. You were a beast."

The way my pants fit is sublime. We got them off the sale rack. My mom convinced me to go a size up and said, "Honey, you have nothing to worry about, you look great." The way they don't cut into me, even after the pizza, is amazing.

"We've never been worried about you, honey," says my mom.

"Oh fuck no," says my dad.

On the drive home, I lie down in the back seat. The seat belt twists around my guts. I'm slightly drunk, and I watch the streetlights pass above my head. These beautiful people always keep a box of tissues in the back seat of their car. Their politeness and rightness, to me, in this moment, is boundless.

The next day is my day with my dad. We go for a walk in the woods. The air is so fresh it cracks my face. I want it to crack straight open so that there's no barrier between me and the iced-over creek, the dead trees, the chirping squirrels. We find deer turds, and I put a pretty rock into the pocket of my new peacoat. We get hungry and go home to eat grilled cheese. That night, I look for jobs on my mom's laptop, knowing I have to leave in the morning. I find three positions and email them to myself to inspect on my return.

In the morning, my mom gets out an old backpack of mine from high school and gives it to me as a suitcase. On the train, I notice the bag of chocolate-covered pretzels and a Ziploc bag of almonds inside, and I eat them until they're gone.

chapter 26

I return to my apartment, which is completely in shambles. It didn't look this insane to me before my trip. I get to work, cleaning (I always seem to be cleaning).

I feel instantly depressed. I send out my résumé to three local nonprofits and think about asking Sarah for a recommendation letter. The ballet is hiring people to sell season tickets. I see the ad on Craigslist and reply by leaving an introductory voice mail as instructed.

My phone rings almost immediately after I leave the message. The woman on the line says she liked the way I left my message, how professional and official and polite I'd sounded. I think that she sounds very aggressive and a little threatening, but I appreciate the compliments.

We talk about my availability and have a cursory discussion about my work history (yes, I've used a phone before), and then she tells me about the excitement of sales. I'm told

I can come in tomorrow for an in-person assessment and training, on the spot.

I'm hired.

The next morning, I put on the work outfit my mother bought me, my new coat, my fashion stocking cap and gloves, and go to the ballet offices downtown. A very elegant woman sits in the lobby. Wealthy-looking people mill around. I feel at ease, comfortable. Things will be okay. I've always thought that I could work any job as long as I like the organization I'm working for. I imagine saying this to my new supervisor.

On the elevator, I am the last to leave. I get off on the twelfth floor. The doors open onto a beige hallway with stained gray carpeting and a drop ceiling. There are copiers in the hall. On my immediate left is a break room. The hallway smells like dust and yogurt. I see a woman in an ill-fitting patterned blouse hunching over a cup of Dannon, staring at the wood-patterned laminate table. I gird myself, take a breath, and walk down the hall, noticing the framed posters of past productions, some of them historic and recognizable.

I pass a woman. She's chewing gum. She looks at me but says nothing. I go down to the end of the hall and enter the sales room. Something is beginning to dawn on me, but not quite yet.

In the room, six people sit in cubicles, backs to each other, muttering into headsets. In a dark, glass booth at the far end of the room, I see the outline of a woman in her late fifties, eating a sandwich. I walk to the booth, knock on the glass, and say hello. She raises a finger at me, finishes another bite of her sandwich, and wipes a creamy substance from between her fingers with a patterned Dixie napkin.

She rises, and I offer my hand. She bears down on it too hard, obviously not understanding what a "firm" handshake is, not knowing that a person can overcompensate and seem as ill-fit for business as the limp-handed. I smile and try to correct my attitude.

"I love the posters in the hallway," I say. "It's exciting to be here."

She looks at me like she hates me and asks me again how many hours I can work, and if I have any sales experience, as if we hadn't already been over that on the phone. She wipes the mouthpiece of a headset with a Lysol wipe and hands it to me. She's still chewing. She directs me to a cubicle next to Craig, one of their top earners, and hands me a script.

"I'll have you shadow and train for a week at half pay. Once you start making calls, pay is $7.50 an hour plus commission. You'll be making about twelve, fifteen an hour once you start getting commissions."

"Oh, okay," I say.

"The reason I like you is you sound like the right kind of person to be making these calls."

"Oh, thank you," I say.

"The people on these lists are people who have bought tickets to the ballet before but haven't remembered to get their passes for next season."

She explains that people can hear a smile, so I have to smile while I'm talking.

"Can you say something to me?"

"Oh, um . . ."

"No, that is incorrect. Say 'Hello, I'm calling for Ms. Butler, is she available?'"

I shift. "Uh."

"No."

"Okay. 'Hello, I'm calling for Ms. Butler.'" I feel like I should be embarrassed, but no one seems to notice.

"That's a great example of how not to make a call. I want you to smile and say 'Hello, I'm calling for Ms. Butler, is she available?'"

I do my best, but it takes three more tries. She tells me I have to lose my little-girl attitude and then tells me that no is not in my vocabulary when I'm in this room. I have to pretend that it's a "foreign-language word." I look around and see that everyone is smiling and talking, and she snaps her fingers in my face and tells me that when she's talking, she needs my eyes on hers.

I spend the rest of my three-hour shift sitting behind Craig, listening to his calls.

Craig looks so fragile to me, his stomach sitting in his lap, his tie tucked into his shirt. My supervisor comes up behind me and pushes my chair closer to Craig, so that my knees touch the part of his ass that sticks out of the back of his chair.

I am asked to come back the next day.

I call my mom and try to make a joke of it, not telling her my hourly earnings. I look for something else I could do for work but feel unqualified for everything interesting and repulsed by everything else.

I text Sarah and tell her, haha, to let me know if she quits her job, because I'd like to apply. She tells me I'd hate working in that fucking hellhole.

I make the mistake of asking for free passes to the one-time-only restaging of *The Rite of Spring*, saying, I'm ashamed to admit, *breathlessly*, how I used to listen to a tape of it every night when I was a toddler, and how I had a whole narrative attached to it.

My supervisor looks at me with nothing, no emotion in her face, and says that she'll see what she can do, but not to expect too much, since I'm not even done with my training, and she doesn't know if I'll make it, doesn't know if I have the stuff yet.

The cassette I had of *The Rite of Spring* had a toucan, a giraffe, and a gorilla on the cover, and when I would listen to it, I would imagine being chased by the gorilla through the backyards in my neighborhood, a frantic scramble, hopping fences and hiding, but the story always ended with me safe in my bed, falling asleep.

We do a mock call. My supervisor plays the role of a disinterested potential sale. My cell phone starts ringing during our performance, and my supervisor, like some kind of genius, rolls with it, and asks me what that sound is in the background. She tells me I'm very rude, and that I should stop calling this number. I silence my phone and say, "Okay, ma'am, I'm sorry for the inconvenience, but please do keep us in mind for your future cultural experiences here in Chicago." My neck flushes, and my supervisor says, "I thought no wasn't in your vocabulary," and I say, "I'm sorry, it's difficult for me to playact." She says there are people who are literally fighting for my job, and I should let her know if I can't handle it. I apologize.

She has me role-play with Craig for an hour.

I leave work at 2:00 each day and eat two pieces of pizza from the 7-Eleven on my walk home. Sometimes I take an Uber, sometimes I walk, but I never take the train. Something about it. I like to feel either cold and tired or warm and safe. I get in bed, often in my work clothes, and fall asleep immediately.

I look at a chair that I never sit in, a vintage armchair with nubbled, pea-green upholstery. I could sell that chair for two to three hundred dollars. So far, I've made sixty dollars, before tax, at the call center. I walk up to the chair and mimic vomiting on it, and then kick it. Snow falls.

I need someone, so I make plans with Sarah. We've been texting a bit, and she knows about my new job. I want to feel the way I used to feel. Even that grinding, deadening, pseudo nine-to-five bullshit would be better. I tell her I'm having my first sales day today (wish me luck!) and she doesn't respond. I stress eat a Danish.

I arrive at the call center and feel the anxiety vomit inside of me. I look at my new coworkers—a woman who weighs maybe ninety pounds, dressed like a ballerina, somewhere between forty and sixty years of age, two teens, Craig, a nervous, laughing man named Randy, the hallway gum chewer, the yogurt eater, and my supervisor. Over the past week and a half, I learned where they all came from— "artists," office workers who were looking for more salary on the side (questionable), GEDs, rejects, born agains.

I put on my headset and look at my script. I hit the first phone number and compulsively click the next call button after two rings. I mark the person as not at home. The next woman says, "No, I'm sorry, she's not at home right now, can I take a message?" even though I'm certain it's her, and when I ask if she might have any interest in the ballet, she laughs and hangs up. The next guy shouts at me and hangs up. Most calls go straight to voice mail.

I can feel my supervisor standing behind me.

My muscles tense.

I'm on the phone with a man who sounds like my father. He's explaining, very calmly, that he's asked to be taken off the call list four times now, but he keeps getting these calls, and no offense to the ballet, but it's getting ridiculous. My supervisor asks me if I'm smiling and if I have no in my vocabulary.

"Look at that area code, that's *North Shore*. Ask him if he has enough money to support our season."

I'm trying to listen to him, but she keeps shouting in my ear, stepping closer to me, and I say, "Sorry about that, there must be something wrong with our data." He tells me he knows it's not my fault, but he's angry, fed up, and I can hear my supervisor laugh and say, "There's nothing wrong with our data," and I'm listening to her, and I'm listening to him, and I put my finger in my ear to concentrate on what he's saying, because I really can't hear him over her laughing and shouting. And then my supervisor leans over me and runs her fingers along my cheek and sweeps back my hair. Because of my new haircut, I can feel it all the way up into my scalp. My whole body shudders. She pulls on my hair, very slightly, but the tug is there, the anger is there. My blocked ear is exposed, and she gets mad and shouts, "Don't plug your ear to me!" I tell the man (wondering if he can hear what's going on) that I'll get things straightened out, have a nice day, and I hang up, feeling frozen and shocked. My supervisor tells me that I am *never* to close my ear to her when she's speaking to me. I try to explain that it's difficult to carry on two conversations at once, and she tells me that that's a skill I'll need to develop. "Everyone here has learned it." Then she insults my intelligence, and I can still feel the hand she laid on me, the tug on my scalp, and I say I'm going to use the restroom, and leave the building, forever.

chapter 27

I can identify one of my major problems in life as follow-through, or lack of follow-through. I plan to bring this up with Sarah, hoping we can talk about it, so that I can come to some kind of conclusion about everything. I'm jumpy and pacing the apartment.

I haven't seen Sarah in more than a month, not since I lost my job at the showroom, which I'm hoping she'll understand.

On my walk home from the call center I bought a twelve-pack of Goose Island 312. Appropriate. Funny. I have ten missed calls from a Chicago area code.

I open a beer and keep pacing. I could probably return to the call center tomorrow, play off my absence as a misinterpretation of my schedule. My phone rings again, for fuck's sake, this time going to voice mail. I remember a college boyfriend who said something like, "If you're going to do something at all, you have to do it really well." He probably read that somewhere. What did he know?

I try to assess the things that bring me pleasure, and how those things might bring me a fulfilling career. I think about how I spend my time. Where my interests lie. The questions come naturally, as if supplied by the ether, and the answer sits in my empty skull: nothing. Nothing, nothing, nothing.

Sarah buzzes. She's brought her normal offering of two warm PBRs still attached to the rings, and I offer her a 312, so that hers can cool in the fridge. She doesn't ask me how I'm doing.

Sarah asserts that she thought she should have brought some beer since I'm hosting. She asks if I have cigarettes.

"I had a kind of fucked up day at work," I say.

Sarah nods. "Yeah, my shit's always fucked up." She tells me about how her office mate is always listening to shitty music, and how she can feel a confrontation brewing.

"Well, you know. Just choose your words wisely, and re-member to pick your battles," I say. "Just be careful when you're dealing with sensitive people. You know, you just don't want to end up—"

"With a shitty job like yours?" she says.

"Yeah."

I drink.

"Yeah, well, don't worry about that," she says. "I don't think it'll ever come down to a call center for me."

"Yeah, of course," I say, not even angry yet. That always comes later.

We drink.

"So you said today was shitty or something?" says Sarah. It comes out forced, like she's just reminded herself to ask about me.

"Yeah, it was exceptionally bad."

Sarah shrugs.

"I made my first calls today. It was a singular experience."

"Yeah, I feel like that would be pretty shitty. My friend Chloe used to do call center work and she said people would yell at her all the time, but she was pretty good at it, and she made some bank. But she was really personable and had a good sense of humor about it."

"Yeah, well, it wasn't so much the calling part. My supervisor pulled my hair."

Sarah seems strangely unimpressed. I explain myself in more detail, going back to the beginning, the role playing, the aggression, and the yelling that led to the hair pulling.

"I left after that," I say.

"Did you tell her you were leaving?"

"No, I just couldn't deal with it. Nobody's ever actually physically touched me at work before."

"So you're unemployed again?"

I say, "Yeah, I guess so," at a strangely loud volume, and we continue to drink.

Sarah says she wishes she could just quit her job, I guess implying that I'm lucky.

We talk for a minute about how I didn't get the job at the showroom, and Sarah tells me that's just the way those temp jobs go.

"Right, I know. I just feel like I'm at an impasse. I don't know what to do."

"You should stop quitting your jobs," she says. "That would help. Probably don't steal shit from your jobs anymore, either."

I pretend I didn't hear that last thing, so irrelevant, so cruel.

She says something else about her job, some story where some person tried and failed to make her feel a certain, unflattering, way about herself. My pulse goes up, and I say, "Damn, that sucks."

I just want to sit on the couch and watch a movie and order some food, which seems so infuriatingly simple and doable, but also objectively, at this point, impossible.

I want her to say, "Oh, Millie, you're fine—this is really common. Look at you, you're so smart, you're really great, the economy is really bad right now. People post about job openings all the time. If you can just make it one more month, I know you'll find something. This will pass. Don't be so hard on yourself."

I finish my beer and say, "Well, aren't we a pair?"

"It's not exactly the same situation," she says.

"Totally," I say.

I get another beer. We keep drinking. Keep shooting the breeze.

I get socked in the chest, thinking about how things never change. How they're on a slow-rolling slope downward, and you can think up a long list of things you'd rather do, but because of some kind of inertia, or hard facts about who you are and what life is, you always end up back where you started, sitting drunk on a hard, sticky chair with someone you hate.

Sarah is talking about how she might go public about the toxicity in her workplace.

"Would you do that while you're still there?" I ask.

The sound of her voice is like nails on a chalkboard. Like putting my hand in a garbage disposal. I feel like I might snap if she keeps talking. I can feel the beginnings of an insane, unbridled laugh stirring inside me. She shoots me a look and says she's not going to leave the job. She's going to try to get her boss fired by the board. I ask her if she thinks she'd apply for her boss's position, and she can't even tell that I'm joking.

"I'm worried I'm getting seriously depressed again," I say.

Sarah gets another one of my beers and another one of my cigarettes and says, "Yeah, me too."

"Oh no, I hope you're going to be okay," I say, eyes wide with undisguised hostility.

"I'll pull out of it," she says.

We go through several more beers and she groans and tells me she needs to lie down. She gets down on my floor, and the thick, rubber soles of her boots get caught in my pink rag rug, the one I bought in college and have been using ever since. There's dirty water on the bottoms of her boots, and it turns the soft fibers a grimy, fleshy color.

I get down on the floor and stare at her. "Take your fucking shoes off when you're in my home."

Sarah sighs and says, "Give me a break."

I tell her I'm dead serious and she groans, annoyed. I pull one of her boots off and throw it into the corner and she laughs. I feel myself riding the line between convivial faux anger and actual rage.

I grab her other boot, pull it off, and set it down next to me. She laughs again and tries to pull her foot away, but I have her by the ankle, and my grip is firm.

"Your feet reek," I say.

"No, they don't."

"Oh, really?" I say. I take her foot and move it up to her nose, and she starts laughing.

Finally we're getting somewhere, having some kind of fun.

"Okay, I guess they do stink, but it's winter. Everybody's feet stink in winter."

"No, they don't," I say, and I put my foot on her face. I can feel her nose, the cartilage, through my tights.

Sarah laughs and says, "What the fuck?"

If someone were to see us, they would say, "Oh, look at those two, at it again!"

I sit back down on the floor and smell my own foot. Woolite. I reach up to the table for her beer, hand it to her, and she drinks from it, still lying down. It runs down the side of her face and into her ears and she laughs again, apparently having a good time. I sit Indian style and drink, looking down at her.

"I smell good. I'm really clean," I say.

"We smell the same," she says.

I close my eyes and breathe through my nose and I want to scream. I tell her I've taken great pains to smell this way.

"Oh, uh-huh, okay, Millie."

I get up on my knees and waddle over to her. I put my armpit on her face and say, "See??"

I acknowledge that I press my armpit on her face a bit too

hard. She says, "Okay, okay, you win, Jesus, stop being so fucking ridiculous."

"I have had hands lain upon me at the workplace!" I shout, trying to make some kind of joke about the spiritual laying of hands, the transformation that's supposed to follow, and how no one leaves a job unchanged, but it falls flat. There's too much unspoken context. "I'm a reject of society," I say.

"Oh my god, look around you," she says.

I assume this is in reference to all my stuff—the mid-mod clamp light above my stove, my Swedish Technivorm coffeemaker, the wine-colored blouse that my mother bought me, etc. etc. I light a cigarette and wave my hand around dismissively.

"Not me," I say, and she laughs again, but this time I don't feel included in it. "I have a criminal's heart," I say, wishing it were true.

"You do not have a criminal's heart," she says. There's no note of condolence in her delivery, only anger.

I want to rewind a few of the beers and watch a movie on the couch. I want her to borrow my new pajamas and have a slumber party with me, *god dammit*, but instead she's bickering with me about how easy I have it, and how I'm not a reject or a criminal, and it's so fucking frustrating, so boring, I could die.

My head spins a little from the beer.

Sarah's talking, but I'm used to tuning her out, used to thinking that what she has to offer me, conversationally, is completely worthless.

I think about Tiffany and the Etch A Sketch. Impossible,

but I think I can still feel her neck in my hands. I think about the yoga class. The soaps I wanted to buy for my mom. I think about telling Sarah to get the fuck out of my house. I would shout it in some kind of demonic baritone, *"GET THE FOCK OUT OF MY HOUSE!!!"* I think about how every decision I make is a no, how every act is essentially a no, and I feel tears welling in my chest and face, and I think about how even if I let them out it wouldn't make a fucking difference. The answer is still always no, eternally no. I want to slap Sarah. I'm in striking range. I want to spit in her face and scream, but it wouldn't matter.

I stand, give her a soft kick in the shoulder, open another beer, and change the subject.

"So, how's shit with Chris?"

I sit in my chair with my legs crossed at the knee and try to keep as physically still as possible. The evening ends when the beers are gone.

chapter 28

Time moved on in a fucking blur. Years passed. The river where Millie was fired from her middling job at the temp agency continued to flow, on and on, eventually overrun by carp, as predicted, the corpses of the carp laughed at, squealed at, and pushed aside by the oars of tourists on kayaks. People still bought season passes to the ballet, hoping that the performances would somehow transform them. Resolutions were made, resolutions were broken. People took comfort, unknowingly, in the anger that filled them, the anger that took them out of themselves and into another dimension—a hallucination of the perfect future. No one thought about the scope of history that would evade them, the sea of identical people who would replace them as time made its waves back and forth, back and forth, seemingly linear, deceptive, stationary and changing all at once.

Somewhere in the circle of Millie's time on Earth, she

spent a sleepless night mulling things over. She was no longer in the part of life where things changed. Her actions from here on out would carry more permanence, could no longer be easily swapped out for something new. Realizing this, she felt panic, deep and wide and boundless, and then she felt release.

Millie stood from her desk and leaned backward, feeling all the muscles along her spine compress and relax.

She yawned, tried to muffle the sound in her mouth, but eventually let out a high, caricatured sigh. Alyssa, in the next cubicle, silently mimicked the sound (which she found disgustingly self-satisfied, musical, almost like Millie was saying "Yum-yum-yum"). To Alyssa, Millie was a cautionary thing, a reminder not to stay in the same job for too long. Millie's title, "Junior Office Manager," repulsed her completely. Alyssa was going to grad school, for sure, probably in New York. Everything between now and then was biding time.

Millie's shoe was cutting into her heel, and she couldn't remember if she still had Band-Aids at home. She slipped her foot out of her shoe and hit print on the spreadsheet.

On her way to the printer, she stopped and asked Alyssa if she was looking forward to the weekend.

"Yup."

"Me too."

The sheets came out of the printer warm, and Millie pressed them to her cheek, very briefly, as she walked along the hallway to Claire's office.

She overshot Claire's door by a few feet, pivoted on her heel, said "Whoops!" and walked back.

She knocked before opening the door.

Claire, thirty-two years old and the office manager proper, had the obligatory framed family photos next to her Dell monitor and often listened to a Top 40s playlist at a very low volume.

"Hey, Millie, what's up?" she said.

"I have this for you," said Millie, handing over the papers.

"You are actually the best, thank you so much."

Millie smiled.

"Did you want me to adjust the portal today, or would Monday be okay for that?"

"Oh, Monday—Monday is totally fine," said Claire. She was thumbing through the spreadsheets out of habit, not out of a need to check the work. Millie was still standing there in the doorway.

"Oh my gosh, I'm sorry, I'm totally spacing," said Claire. "Were you hoping to take off a little early today?"

"If it's all the same to you."

"You got some big weekend plans?" asked Claire.

"Nothing really. I'm just going to relax."

Claire smiled and said, "Yeah, go ahead, take off. I wish I could have a relaxing weekend to myself!"

Claire winced, embarrassed by her verbalized assumption that Millie was alone.

Millie turned off her computer, said good-bye to Alyssa, and walked out of the building toward the train platform. The summer breeze moved the leaves in the most perfect way. Friday. Blissfully free. The vast expanse of hours laid out in front of her. The countless hours between now and the end.

Acknowledgments

Endless gratitude to my editor, Lindsey Schwoeri, and my agent, Claudia Ballard, for their time and dedication to this book. And, as always, thank you to Emma, Sooze, Jerz, Babby, Mom, and Dad.